Where The Boats Are

By J. A. Baumhofer

© 2002 by J. A. Baumhofer

REVISED EDITION

Published by
Little River Books Division
J. R. Simpson & Associates, Inc.
2175 Huntington Drive
Florissant, Missouri 63033-1227

Telephone 314-921-4419

Manufactured in the United States of America

Library of Congress Control Number 2002106425

ISBN 0-9703086-2-0

Where The Boats Are

By

J. A. Baumhofer

A Little River Book

Dedication

This edition of *Where The Boats Are* is dedicated to the memory of my parents, Jim and Helen Baumhofer, and to my grandmother, Emma Langdon.

Illustrations

Illustrations (Cont.)

Foreword

It has been over ten years since my first modest edition of WHERE THE BOATS ARE came off the press. Many of my loyal readers have bought copies of every edition, and I have often been extremely surprised and gratified by your praise and kind comments.

From the start, this book has been a "labor of love," born out of my lifelong devotion to Lake Superior and her boats. Growing up in St. Paul, I would eagerly await family trips to my grandmother's house in Duluth. There, in her tiny house on the Point of Rocks, I would hope for fog, so I could lie awake at night listening to the foghorn's drone and the boats' answering whistles.

Back then, in the 1960s and early 70s, the harbor and shipping in general was much more prominent in the Twin Ports than today. Most of Duluth and Superior's development (except for tourism) has been away from the harbor. For someone like myself, used to prowling around the waterfront in those days, today's Canal Park is a different world. Some of the changes, like the Marine Museum, Lakewalk and Vista Fleet, have been great. Others, such as the glitzy hotels and restaurants that line the waterfront and obstruct the view of the lake, do very little for me. But, change is the natural way of things. The next time you're down at the Aerial Bridge, imagine this: no hotels, no restaurants, no manicured flower beds, no rollerblades or bike riders. Instead visualize old warehouse buildings, streets with some grime and "atmosphere," and a steady procession of small, straight deck boats whistling for the bridge, often as many as ten per hour. That's the way it was!

Anyway, enough of my reminiscing. Welcome to this new and improved version of WHERE THE BOATS ARE! There are several new features in this edition, including the ten most watchable lake boats. Thanks for your support through the years, and enjoy!

J. A. Baumhofer

Contents

J. A. Baumhofer

Introduction

The deep blast of a whistle pierces the cool Lake Superior air—one long, one short; one long, one short. Then the answering horn of the Aerial Lift Bridge, higher but penetrating. Under the bridge, a streamlined lake boat glides in or out of Duluth harbor. This scene of the long boats passing is repeated night and day for nearly ten months of the year, on glorious summer days when the sun is warm and the breeze cool, and on freezing gray days when the "gales of November" reign. Not often thought of by the casual observer as things of beauty, these huge lake boats are really monuments to our industrial efficiency. They transport the bulk materials that help produce our new cars, warm and light our homes, and even feed us. And still, they can be beautiful!

Some may feel that many of the newer boats lack the charm and appeal of the older lakers. However, what they may lack in charm is made up in their sheer, awesome size. Some over 1000 feet long, these high tech "super Lakers" can carry close to 70,000 tons of iron ore or coal. The Twin Ports of Duluth and Superior ship enough iron ore in these boats each year to make the steel used in 4.7 million cars; the ore cargo of a single 1000-foot freighter is enough for the steel for 16,000 new cars! The low sulphur coal that is shipped from the Midwest Energy Terminal in Superior each year is enough to supply a year's worth of electric power to every household in Michigan, its chief destination. And, the total grain storage capacity of the port's grain elevators would be enough to feed every person in Minnesota for six years!

People from all walks of life share a mutual interest in watching the ever changing activity of the harbor. In the summer, there are usually hundreds of waving, camera-toting boatwatchers lining the piers of the Duluth ship canal. At other times, when snow and ice descend on Lake Superior, there may be only a handful. But, they are always

Crowds of tourists watch the incoming COURTNEY BURTON at Canal Park.

there, and the thrill never goes away. Ever since shipping on the lakes began, Great Lakes boats (and that's what traditionalists always call them) have fascinated people across the region. All boatwatching sites discussed in this book are shown on the maps. The maps are not drawn to scale or intended to be street maps, but just to give an idea of the routes to take to see the boats. As you read, I will take you on your very own boatwatching tour of the Twin Ports and Lakehead. The Duluth Superior tour is first. Starting at Canal Park, it is possible to visit the sites in one long loop, as they are numbered consecutively. Of course, there will probably never be a time with boats at all the areas. Then you can just omit this area from your tour and go on to the next. Before starting to explore, it's a good idea to stop at one of the several visitor centers near downtown for a street map, brochures about other attractions, etc.

The best way to start checking on boat activity is by calling the "Boatwatcher's Hotline" at (218) 722-6489. This recorded message is provided by the Canal Park Marine Museum and Visitor Center. A 24-hour line during the shipping season, it gives details on boat traffic in the harbor, plus what is expected. However, the Hotline isn't always 100% accurate, and it's sometimes more fun to look for the boats on your own. This book shows you how! There is also a complete listing of all U. S. and Canadian boats, harbor statistics and historical data, boatwatching tools, and more. There are some interesting museums in the Twin Ports for the boat buff. The Canal Park Marine Museum 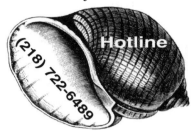 in Duluth is a must. The starting point of our tour, their many excellent displays depict all phases of Great Lakes shipping. The Marine Museum also features a viewing area of the lake, a staffed information booth, and a video bulletin board showing the day's expected boat traffic. Superior boasts an interesting museum boat. The only surviving example of the unique whaleback freighters, which were designed and built by Twin Ports native Alexander McDougall, is located at Barker's Island. The METEOR, built in Superior in 1896, is a great example of these boats of a bygone era.

Also in this book, we will head north for a special boatwatching tour of the Canadian Lakehead, Thunder Bay, Ontario. One of the largest ports in Canada, Thunder Bay is sometimes overlooked by boatwatchers because less emphasis is placed on the harbor here than in the Twin Ports. However, I will show you many out of the way spots that will help make your Thunder Bay visit really rewarding.

The Duluth-Superior Harbor

Though hampered by the northern winter, the Twin Ports are still among the top ten in the U. S. in tonnage, and the largest American port on the Great Lakes. Most years, over 35 million tons of cargo are shipped here, and the tonnage was even greater in years past. Over 7,500 acres in size, the harbor has 49 miles of frontage, and 17 miles of dredged and maintained ship channels. These are kept at the 27 foot depth that is standard throughout the St. Lawrence Seaway, for which the harbor is the western terminus. During the April to December average shipping season, the port moves millions of tons of taconite (iron ore) pellets to steel mills in the lower Great Lakes; millions of tons of low sulphur western coal to power plants in Michigan, Canada and elsewhere; and millions of bushels of grain, mainly for export. Incoming cargoes include large quantities of Michigan limestone; salt for highway use; and a variety of general cargoes.

Twin Ports harbor on a Busy Day.

4

The Twin Ports harbor is a busy place! Close to 1,000 lake boats visit the harbor annually, along with many foreign saltwater ships, called "salties." Saltie visits fluctuate due to a number of factors, but there are usually around 200 of them in a normal season.

The first waterfront development in Duluth was on the lakeshore, outside the harbor, near the foot of present-day Fourth Avenue East. However, when the effects of the fall gales were first felt, these early docks were soon abandoned, and subsequent activity took place in the inner harbor. The only natural entrance to the harbor is through the Superior piers. Excavation of the Duluth harbor entrance in 1871 was challenged in court by Superior, and they were able to obtain a court order stopping the work. However, before the injunction reached Duluth, the ship canal was almost complete, due in part to an all out effort by local residents. In August of that year, the first boat glided through the newly constructed piers. Also, in 1870, the Lake Superior & Mississippi Railroad had been built, connecting the head of the lakes with St. Paul and points east. The first harbor elevators and docks were built in the 1870s and 1880s, mainly on the waterfront near today's Railroad Street, and along Rice's Point adjacent to Garfield Avenue. By 1900, with the tremendous boom of iron ore on the Mesabi Range, shipments from the port were already reaching large proportions.

The 1940s will probably always be remembered as the peak years for cargo tonnage and boat activity. During these war years, there were sometimes over 10,000 vessel calls in a single year! On November 9, 1943, there were an amazing 39 boat arrivals and 53 departures, with a minimum of 63 boats in the harbor at any one time that day! As active as the harbor can be even today, this would be hard to imagine. It may take awhile to digest all these statistics. What they really add up to is a working harbor that is a valuable asset to the community and our country. The most unique thing about the harbor is that it combines all aspects of a working port and a recreational area. Sailing regattas and charter fishing boats can co-exist with thousand foot freighters, for the benefit of all.

Duluth Aerial Bridge.

ABOUT THE AERIAL BRIDGE

The Duluth Aerial Bridge is one of the Great Lakes' most well known landmarks. Built in 1905, the bridge originally carried passengers and vehicles across the canal in a gondola type car that was pulled from one side to the other. Changed to its current configuration in 1929, the bridge can rise to its full height of 138 feet in only 55 seconds. The Aerial Bridge has a span length of 386 feet, with a distance of 172 feet from the water to the lower edge of the truss, and 22.7 feet from the water to the upper edge. The 900-ton lift span is counterbalanced by two 450-ton concrete blocks, one at each side of the lift span.

STORMS AND WRECKS

The Twin Ports have seen their share of interesting and dramatic weather events. Winter's ice often lasts well into the spring on Lake Superior. One of the best known "ice years" was 1917, when boats were trapped for days at a time in May, sometimes in danger of running out of food and supplies. As late as June 6 of that year, fourteen boats were trapped in thick ice off the Duluth piers. The latest breakup ever of the harbor ice was in 1876, when ice lasted until

June 28! As recently as 1991, several boats (including thousand footers) were trapped in early April. At that time, it took the Coast Guard icebreaker MACKINAW and several other cutters to free them.

Also well known among mariners are Lake Superior's infamous storms. Perhaps the worst of the "gales of November" here was on the 27th and 28th of the month in 1905. That storm combined heavy snow, below zero temperatures, and a twelve-hour stretch with continuous winds of over 60 miles per hour! In all, eighteen boats were lost. The Str. R.W. ENGLAND was blown ashore 22 miles from Minnesota Point, the ISAAC ELLWOOD was so badly damaged from hitting the piers upon arrival that she sank just inside the harbor, and several others were lost on the North Shore. The most well known shipwreck from this storm was the MATAAFA. She struck the north pier while trying to enter the harbor, then broke in half with the loss of nine crewmen, all within sight of many spectators at what is now Canal Park. Of course, the Twin Ports played a well known part in Lake Superior's most recent (and probably best known) shipwreck. The EDMUND FITZGERALD had loaded taconite pellets at the Burlington Northern ore dock in Superior just before sinking with all hands on November 10, 1975, on the eastern end of the lake.

Thunder Bay has also had its share of storms, wrecks and accidents. The 1905 storm that wreaked havoc in the Twin Ports was also felt here. The Str. MONKSHAVEN was blown onto the rocks of Angus Island near Thunder Cape November 28. The crew were more fortunate than those on the MATAAFA however, and were all rescued after spending an entire day and night in the cold on Pie Island. On June 21, 1953, the Paterson Str. SCOTIADOC was departing the harbour in heavy fog. With 50 mile per hour winds and visibility near zero, she was rammed by the Str. BURLINGTON, and sank with a full cargo of wheat. All of the crew except one were rescued by the BURLINGTON. These and many others like them are the stories of Lake Superior. To see the lake on a warm summer day (as many visitors do) makes it very difficult to imagine the fall gales, winter ice, and spring fogs that have affected the boats so much through the years.

OTHER DIVERSIONS

During your Twin Ports visit, you may want to enjoy some of the many other attractions the area has to offer. The Depot Museum, William A. Irvin, historic Glensheen mansion and the Lakewalk are well known, and can be easily found in popular visitor guides. I will just list a couple lesser known personal favorites.

At the western end of Duluth, historic Fond du Lac is an interesting spot. Site of the first permanent settlements in the region, French traders operated here as early as 1784. John Jacob Astor's American Fur Company built a trading post and fort here in 1809. Now Fond du Lac is a sleepy Duluth suburb about 15 miles southwest of downtown. It is reached by taking I-35 south from town to the Grand Avenue exit. Grand Avenue becomes State Highway 23, which you can follow to Fond du Lac on the St. Louis River. The best place to stop is at Chamber's Grove Park, which is near the site of the old trading post, and has scenic views of the river.

Skyline Drive, mentioned later in the book, has a little known and very scenic western section. To reach it, start at the Spirit Mountain ski area, at the top of the hill, off of Boundary Avenue and I-35. After exiting, cross over the freeway and follow the signs for Skyline Drive. Part of this road is unpaved, but there is spectacular scenery overlooking western Duluth and the St. Louis River estuary with its many islands and inlets. There are frequent turnoffs where you can stop for viewing and photography. During the peak of fall foliage color, about October 1, this is a truly awesome drive. You can continue on Skyline for several miles until it ends at Becks Rd. Turn left here, and continue past more spectacular scenery back to Highway 23 in the Gary neighborhood. You can turn left here and return to the freeway and downtown, or turn right to visit Fond du Lac.

J. A. Baumhofer

CARGOES OF THE TWIN PORTS

The rich iron mines of Minnesota have long provided the impetus for much of the shipping activity at the Twin Ports, and on the lakes in general. Since the 1960s, most of the ore shipped has been in the form of taconite pellets, which are produced from a lower grade of ore than was originally used. Lately, with the sharp rise in steel imports and economic ups and downs, ore shipments have fluctuated. However, over ten million tons are normally shipped each year, and the Burlington Northern ore docks in Superior remain among the largest on the lakes.

The grain trade is another of the port's mainstays. Small amounts of Twin Ports grain are shipped domestically, usually to Buffalo, New York. Most grain is exported. Some Canadian exports stay in Canada, but most are carried through the St. Lawrence Seaway for trans-shipment. In this, the grain is transferred to elevators in the lower St. Lawrence River ports of Quebec. There, it is re-loaded onto ocean ships for export. Also, large amounts of grain are loaded onto ocean ships here for direct overseas export. After loading here, these "salties" will top off with additional grain on the St. Lawrence.

The most frequent destinations for Twin Ports grain exports are Europe and North Africa. Grain tonnage loaded here usually amounts to around four million tons yearly. Wheat, corn and soybeans are the grains most commonly handled, but some barley, oats and oil seeds are also shipped.

This brings us to coal, which has recently made news as the leading cargo shipped from the Twin Ports. In the past, coal was almost always an inbound cargo, used for local industrial and utility purposes. But, that has all changed with the advent of low sulphur, western coal electric power. Because of the high demand for this type of coal worldwide due to environmental concerns, coal tonnages have reached surprising volumes. The Midwest Energy Resources Terminal in Superior is continuing to expand their volume, and set a record of 15.1 million tons shipped in 2001. The bulk of this coal is destined for Detroit Edison power plants throughout Michigan, but recently there have been increased shipments to Canada and even some overseas destinations. Western coal has been the bright spot in Twin Ports shipping for the past decade, and there is room for more records to be set.

Among other cargoes, the most important is limestone. Large amounts of Michigan limestone are unloaded at the port's stone docks each year. This stone has many uses, including the manufacture of taconite pellets, the purification of beet sugar, pollution control at power plants, and for many agricultural uses. Other bulk cargoes shipped through the port include dry cement, salt, petroleum coke and Bentonite clay.

In addition to all of these, many unusual and specialized general cargoes are handled at the Port Terminal in Duluth. In the past few years, the Port Terminal has handled paper mill machinery from Sweden bound for Canada, huge oil refinery vessels from Japan for a petroleum project in Canada, and many others. These are often unloaded onto specially designed railcars at the Port Terminal for transfer to their destinations. The large Port Terminal cranes are often put to use for unloading general cargoes of European steel. In an interesting "first," large cargoes of lumber imported from Europe were handled by the port for the first time in 2001.

BOATS YOU MAY SEE

In this section, I have a listing of all U. S. and Canadian lake boats, even though it would be highly unusual to see some of them here. However, in the Twin Ports and Thunder Bay, anything might turn up! This is part of what makes boatwatching so fun and challenging. Traffic patterns on the lakes are such that, what is common or rare at any given time in any year, may be exactly opposite at another. Some boats make what are called dedicated runs, and can be seen at the ore or coal docks every few days. Others may be seen only once or twice a year, or not at all.

The listings are organized by fleet, and there is a capsule history for most of the commonly seen ones. For each boat, there is an abbreviation showing the type of boat, when it was built, dimensions, and cargo capacity. The cargo capacities shown are averages, and can vary greatly due to the season, and other factors. For boats that normally use the St. Lawrence Seaway, the capacity listed is that which conforms to standard Seaway drafts.

At this point, I will briefly discuss the types of boats you will encounter. Self-unloaders are by far the most commonly seen type of boat on the Great Lakes. They are easily identifiable by the large crane-like unloading boom most of them carry on their decks. The great advantage of self-unloaders is the ability they have to unload cargo virtually anywhere, without assistance from onshore unloading equipment. Though in use on a small scale since the early 1900s, they have only come into general use through the development of taconite pellets. Prior to the use of taconite, high grade natural iron ore had a much more soft and loose texture, and was normally always shipped on the straight deck bulk carriers. The hard, round taconite pellet of uniform size made an ideal cargo for self-unloading boats. Before this, self-unloaders were mainly used for carrying coal and limestone.

Straight deck bulk carriers, once the mainstay of Great Lakes shipping, are being seen less often all the time. The KINSMAN INDEPENDENT is the only one left in regular use in the U. S. fleet. They are still more common in the Canadian fleet, but the trend is toward self-unloaders there as well. Most boatwatchers feel the day is coming when the straight decker will be a thing of the past. For this reason, the few that are left are very sought after for photographs, etc.

There are a few other specialized boat types. Cement carriers appear the same as straight deckers, but carry special equipment below deck to handle dry cement cargoes. Tankers on the Great Lakes (now uncommon) handle a variety of liquid bulk cargoes. The newest trend in lake boats are the tug/barges. Often converted from older self-propelled boats, they range in size from the thousand foot PRESQUE ISLE to small tank barges. The newest boat built for Great Lakes service, the GREAT LAKES TRADER of the Van Enkevort Co., is a tug/barge, and you can expect to see more of them over the years. When a boat has been rebuilt in any way, as is often the case, the date given is the date of her new configuration, rather than that of the original launch.

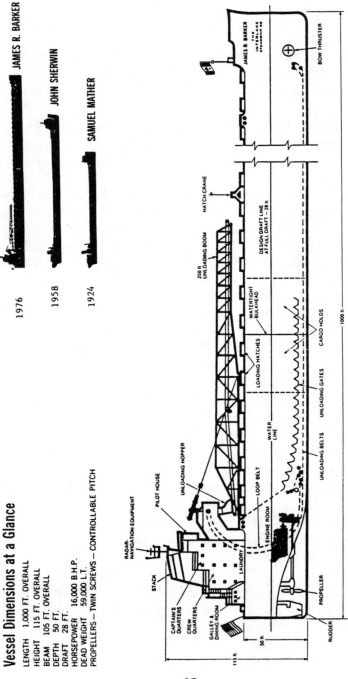

Vessel Dimensions at a Glance

LENGTH   1,000 FT. OVERALL
HEIGHT   115 FT. OVERALL
BEAM   105 FT. OVERALL
DEPTH   50 FT.
DRAFT   28 FT.
HORSEPOWER 16,000 B.H.P.
DEAD WEIGHT 59,000 L.T.
PROPELLERS — TWIN SCREWS — CONTROLLABLE PITCH

JAMES R. BARKER
1976

JOHN SHERWIN
1958

SAMUEL MATHER
1924

BOW THRUSTER

JAMES R. BARKER
THE INTERLAKE STEAMSHIP CO.

HATCH CRANE

250 ft UNLOADING BOOM

DESIGN DRAFT LINE AT FULL DRAFT — 28 ft

WATERTIGHT BULKHEAD

1000 ft

LOADING HATCHES

CARGO HOLDS

WATER LINE

UNLOADING GATES

UNLOADING HOPPER

LOOP BELT

UNLOADING BELTS

ENGINE ROOM

PILOT HOUSE

RADAR-NAVIGATION EQUIPMENT

STACK

CAPTAIN'S QUARTERS

CREW QUARTERS

GALLEY & DINING ROOM

LAUNDRY

PROPELLER

RUDDER

50 ft.

115 ft

Design of a typical 1,000-foot "super Laker" with diagram showing evolution in size of Lake boats.

12

J. A. Baumhofer

ABBREVIATIONS

SU = Self-Unloader   SDB = Straight Deck Bulk

TK = Tanker   CC = Cement Carrier   TB = Tug/Barge

• Denotes Inactive Recently But May Change

ALGOMA CENTRAL MARINE: This company operates one of the oldest fleets in continuous existence on the Great Lakes and Seaway. Founded in 1900, they now have a diverse fleet of self-unloaders, straight deckers and tankers. Algoma is also involved in ocean shipping, and is in a joint venture with Upper Lakes Shipping, where theyhave pooled their boats for greater efficiency.

AGAWA CANYON	SU	1970	21,000	646' x 72' x 40'
AIRD, JOHN B.	SU	1983	27,000	730' x 76' x 46'
ALGOBAY	SU	1978	26,000	730' x 76' x 46'
ALGOCAPE	SDB	1967	26,000	730' x 75' x 40'
ALGOCATAYLYST	TK	1972		431' x 66' x 35'
ALGOCEN	SDB	1968	26.000	730' x 75' x 40'
ALGOEAST	TK	1977		431' x 66' x 35'
ALGOGULF	SDB	1961	25,000	730' x 75' x 39'
ALGOISLE	SDB	1963	25,000	730' x 75' x 39'
ALGOLAKE	SU	1977	27,000	730' x 75' x 46'
ALGOMARINE	SU	1968	25,000	730' x 75' x 40'
ALGONORTH	SDB	1971	24,000	730' x 75' x 43'
ALGONOVA	TK	1968		440' x 60' x 31'

ALGONTARIO	SDB	1960	26,000	730' X 76' x 40'
ALGOPORT	SU	1979	23,000	658' x 76' x 46'
ALGORAIL	SU	1968	20,000	640' x 72' x 40'
ALGORIVER	SDB	1960	25,000	722' x 75' x 39'
ALGOSAR	TK	1974		435' x 74' x 32'
ALGOSOO	SU	1974	27,000	730' x 75' x 44'
ALGOSOUND	SDB	1965	25,000	730' x 75' x 39'
ALGOSTEEL	SU	1966	25,000	730' x 75' x 40'
ALGOWAY	SU	1972	21,000	650' x 72' x 40'
ALGOWOOD	SU	1981	26,000	730' x 76' x 46'
ALGOVILLE	SDB	1967	26,000	730' x 76' x 46'
CRESSWELL, PETER R.	SU	1982	28,000	730' x 76' x 42'
JACKMAN, CAPT. HENRY	SU	1981	26,000	730' x 76' x 42'
SAUNIERE	SU	1970	19,000	643' x 75' x 42'

AMERICAN STEAMSHIP COMPANY: Some of the most commonly seen boats in the Twin Ports belong to this fleet, headquartered in Buffalo, N.Y. A subsidiary of the General American Transportation Co.. (GATX), they are the offshoot of an old Great Lakes shipping firm, Boland & Cornelius. At press time, they are pooling operations with Oglebay Norton.

AMERICAN MARINER	SU	1980	37,000	730' x 78' x 45'
AMERICAN REPUBLIC	SU	1981	22,000	635' x 68' x 40'
BOLAND, JOHN J.	SU	1973	32,000	680' x 78' x 45'
BUFFALO	SU	1978	22,000	635' X 68' X 40'
CORNELIUS, ADAM E.	SU	1973	33,000	680' x 78' x 45'

14

INDIANA HARBOR	SU	1979	70,000	1,000' x 105' x 56'
LAUD, SAM	SU	1975	23,000	635' x 68' x 40'
McCARTHY, WALTER J., JR.	SU	1977	70,000	1000' x 105' x 56'
ST. CLAIR	SU	1976	44,000	770' x 92' x 52'
STINSON, GEORGE A.	SU	1978	65,000	1004' x 105' x 50'
WHITE, H. LEE	SU	1974	35,000	704' x 78' x 45'

BETHLEHEM STEEL CORP.: One of the largest American steelmakers, Bethlehem at one time had a large fleet of ore carriers. At present, they own two of the 1,000-foot super lakers.

BURNS HARBOR	SU	1980	70,000	1000' x 105' x 56'
CORT, STEWART J.	SU	1972	58,000	1000' x 105' x 49'

CANADA STEAMSHIP LINES: This old Canadian firm operates a large fleet of self-unloaders. They are normally easy to see in either harbor.

ATLANTIC ERIE	SU	1985	25,000	736' x 76' x 50'
ATLANTIC HURON	SU	1984	26,000	736' x 76' x 50'
CSL LAURENTIEN	SU	2001	30,500	740' x 78' x 47'
CSL NIAGARA	SU	1999	30,500	740' X 78' X 48'
CSL TADOUSSAC	SU	2000	26,000	730' x 78' x 42'
ENGLISH RIVER	CC	1961	7,450	404' 60' x 36'
FRONTENAC	SU	1968	25,000	730' x 75' x 40'
HALIFAX	SU	1963	23,000	730' x 75' x 39'
MANITOULIN	SU	1966	24,000	730' x 75' x 41'

Where The Boats Are

MARTIN, RT. HON. PAUL J.	SU	1999	34,500	740' x 78' x 48'
NANTICOKE	SU	1980	26,000	730' x 76' x 46'
PARISIEN, JEAN	SU	1977	27,000	730' x 75' x 46'
SPENCER, SARAH	TB	1989	14,700	594' x 72' x 36'

CEMENT TRANSIT COMPANY: This company owns two very old and interesting boats, including the former MEDUSA CHALLENGER, which is one of the oldest on the lakes. Unfortunately, they would be rare here, operating mainly on Lake Michigan.

SOUTHDOWN CHALLENGER	CC	1906	10,000	552' x 56' x 31'
SOUTHDOWN CONQUEST	CC	1937	8,500	437' x 55' x 28'

CLEVELAND TANKERS: Now partially owned by Algoma, this company operates the only U.S. flagged tankers on the Great Lakes. They are seen only rarely.

GEMINI	TK	1978		430' x 65' x 39'
SATURN	TK	1974		384' x 54' x 25'

COASTWISE TRADING COMPANY: This company operates one tank barge, which occasionally delivers petroleum products to the Twin Ports.

MICHIGAN/GREAT LAKES	TB	1982		454' x 60' x 30'

DESGAGNES TRANSPORT: This company's fleet operates mainly in the lower St. Lawrence River area, and very rarely on Lake Superior.

DESGAGNES, AMELIA	SU	1976	7,000	355' x 49' x 30'
DESGAGNES, CATHERINE	SDB	1962	8,000	410' x 56' x 31'
DESGAGNES, CECELIA	SDB	1971	7,500	375' x 55' x 34'

DESGAGNES, MATHILDA	SDB	1959	6,900	360' x 51' x 30'
DESGAGNES, MELISSA	SDB	1975	7,000	355' x 49' x 30'
DESGAGNES, THALASSA	TK	1976		441' x 56' x 32'
PETROLIA DESGAGNES	TK	1975		441' x 56' x 33'

GREAT LAKES ASSOCIATES: This is the former Kinsman Lines, founded by the Steinbrenner family, and one of the oldest on the lakes.

•KINSMAN ENTERPRISE	SDB	1927	16,000	631' x 65' x 33'
KINSMAN INDEPENDENT	SDB	1952	18,000	642' x 67' x 35'

INTERLAKE STEAMSHIP COMPANY: This large fleet is one of the most commonly seen at the Twin Ports and North Shore. Interlake is the continuation of the old Pickands Mather fleet, which once had so many boats.

BARKER, JAMES R.	SU	1976	60,000	1004' x 105' x 50'
BARKER, KAYE E.	SU	1952	25,000	767' x 70' x 36'
BEEGHLY, CHARLES M.	SU	1959	31,000	806' x 75' x 37'
• HOYT, ELTON II	SU	1952	22,000	698' x 70' x 37'
JACKSON, HERBERT C.	SU	1959	23,000	690' x 75' x 37'
MESABI MINER	SU	1977	63,000	1004' x 105' x50'
PATHFINDER	TB	1997	20,000	647' x 70' x 36'
•SHERWIN, JOHN	SDB	1958	31,000	806' x 75' x 37'
TREGURTHA, LEE A.	SU	1942	29,000	826' x 75' x 39'
TREGURTHA, PAUL R.	SU	1981	70,000	1013' x 105' x 56'

INLAND LAKES MANAGEMENT: Formerly the Huron Cement Co. fleet, these distinctive boats are some of the most interesting of the lakes. They also maintain the oldest boat by far on the Great Lakes and probably the world. The E. M. FORD, built in 1998, still boasts her original engine and other equipment. Though not running at present, the FORD can been seen at the cement dock in Saginaw, MI.

ALPENA	CC	1942	13,000	516' x 67' x 35'
•CRAPO, S. T.	CC	1927	8,000	402' x 60' x 29'
•FORD, E. M.	CC	1898	7,000	428' x 50' x 28'
•FORD, J. B.	CC	1904	6,950	440' x 50' x 28'
IGLEHART, J. A. W.	CC	1936	13,000	501' x 68' x 37'
TOWNSEND, PAUL H.	CC	1945	7,850	447' x 50' x 29'

INLAND STEEL COMPANY: Now known as Central Marine Logistics, the fleet was renamed in 1998 when this old American company was sold to foreign interests. It has some of the most "watched" boats on the lakes, including the BLOCK, which is most often seen here.

BLOCK, JOSEPH L.	SU	1976	37,000	728' x 78' x 45'
•RYERSON, EDWARD L.	SDB	1960	27,000	730' x 75' x 39'
SYKES, WILFRED	SU	1949	21,000	678' x 70' x 37'

LOWER LAKES TOWING LIMITED: This company, along with their U.S. flag subsidiary Grand River Navigation, are of interest in that they have acquired several older, well known Great Lakes boats, which are operating under new names. Hopefully, they will be seen more often on Lake Superior.

CALUMET	SU	1929	12,000	604' x 60' 32'
CUYAHOGA	SU	1943	16,000	620' x 60' x 35'

McKEE SONS	TB	1991	18,000	580' x 71' 38'
MAUMEE	SU	1929	12,000	605' x 60' x 32'
MISSISSAGI	SU	1943	15,000	620' x 60' x 35'
SAGINAW	SU	1953	20,000	639' x 72' x 36'

OGLEBAY NORTON COMPANY: Operating the largest U.S. flag fleet on the lakes, Oglebay has a diverse fleet of 1,000-footers, older lakers, and small self-unloaders. They can be seen often at the Head of the Lakes.

ARMCO	SU	1953	25,000	767' x 70' x 36'
BUCKEYE	SU	1952	22,000	698' x 70' x 37'
BURTON, COURTNEY	SU	1953	22,000	690' x 70' x 37'
COLUMBIA STAR	SU	1981	70,000	1000' x 105' x 56'
FRANTZ, JOSEPH H.	SU	1925	13,000	618' x 62' x 32'
MIDDLETOWN	SU	1942	23,000	730' x 75' x 39'
OGLEBAY, EARL W.	SU	1973	19,000	630' x 68' x 37
NORTON, DAVID Z.	SU	1973	19,000	630' x 68' x 37'
OGLEBAY NORTON	SU	1978	70,000	1000' x 105' x 56'
RESERVE	SU	1953	25,000	767' x 70' x 36'
WHITE, FRED R., JR.	SU	1979	23,000	636' x 68' x 40'
WOLVERINE	SU	1974	19,000	630' x 68' x 37'

P & H SHIPPING: This is the Parrish & Heimbecker Grain Co. fleet. In 2001, they were acquired by Canada Steamship Lines. They are easily seen in Thunder Bay, but are quite rare in the Twin Ports.

MAPLEGLEN	SDB	1960	24,000	715' x 75' x 38"
OAKGLEN	SDB	1954	22,000	714' x 70' x 37'

N. M. PATERSON & SONS: Early in 2002, the Paterson Company went out of business, and their boats have been acquired by Canada Steamship Lines. The new names are listed below.

CEDARGLEN	SDB	1959	26,000	730' x 76' x 40'
COMEAUDOC	SDB	1960	25,000	730' x 75' x 38'
TEAKGLEN	SDB	1967	17,000	608' x 62' x 36'
PINEGLEN	SDB	1985	28,000	736' x 76' x 42'

ULS CORPORATION: An acronym for Upper Lakes Shipping, this Canadian fleet is one of the largest on the lakes. Their boats are normally easy to see in both harbors.

CANADIAN CENTURY	SU	1967	27,000	730' x 75' 45'
CANADIAN ENTERPRISE	SU	1979	28,000	730' x 76' x 45'
CANADIAN LEADER	SDB	1967	26,000	730' x 75' x 39'
CANADIAN MARINER	SDB	1963	26,000	731' x 75' x 39'
CANADIAN MINER	SDB	1966	26,000	730' x 75' x 39'
CANADIAN NAVIGATOR	SDB	1967	26,000	730' x 75' x 43'
CANADIAN OLYMPIC	SU	1976	28,000	730' x 75' x 46'
CANADIAN PROGRESS	SU	1968	27,000	730' x 75' x 46'
CANADIAN PROSPECTOR	SDB	1964	26,000	730' x 76' x 40'
CANADIAN PROVIDER	SDB	1963	25,000	730' x 75' x 39'
CANADIAN RANGER	SU	1961	24,000	730' x 75' x 39'

J. A. Baumhofer

Name	Type	Year	Tonnage	Dimensions
CANADIAN TRADER	SDB	1969	26,000	730' x 75' x 40'
CANADIAN TRANSFER	SU	1998	16,000	650' x 60' x 26'
CANADIAN TRANSPORT	SU	1979	27,000	730' x 76' x 46'
CANADIAN VENTURE	SDB	1965	26,000	730' x 75' x 39'
CANADIAN VOYAGER	SDB	1963	25,000	730' x 75' x 39'
•LEITCH, GORDON C.	SDB	1968	25,000	730' x 75' x 42'
MONTREALAIS	SDB	1962	22,000	730' x 75' x 39'
NORRIS, JAMES	SU	1952	18,000	663' x 67' x 35'
QUEBECOIS	SDB	1963	25,000	730' x 75' x 39'
ROMAN, STEPHEN B.	CC	1965	7,600	489' x 56' x 39'
•SEAWAY QUEEN	SDB	1959	24,000	713' x 72' x 37'

USS GREAT LAKES FLEET: This is the old U.S. Steel Co. fleet, still headquartered in Duluth. Once having scores of boats, they now operate a diverse fleet of self-unloaders, including the only 1,000-foot tug/barge PRESQUE ISLE. An important part of Twin Ports maritime history, they are easy to see here and in Two Harbors.

Name	Type	Year	Tonnage	Dimensions
ANDERSON, ARTHUR M.	SU	1952	25,000	767' x 70' x 36'
BLOUGH, ROGER	SU	1972	43,000	858' x 105' x 41'
CALLAWAY, CASON J.	SU	1952	25,000	767' x 70' x 36'
CLARKE, PHILIP R.	SU	1952	25,000	767' x 70' 36'
GOTT, EDWIN H.	SU	1979	70,000	1004' x 105' x 56'
MUNSON, JOHN G.	SU	1952	25,000	768'x 72' x 36'
PRESQUE ISLE	TB	1973	57,000	1000' x 105' x 46'
SPEER, EDGAR B.	SU	1980	70,000	1004' x 105' x 56'

UPPER LAKES TOWING CO.: This company owns a well known former laker, now converted to a tug/barge. It is rarely seen in the Twin Ports.

THOMPSON, JOSEPH H., JR   TB   1990   21,000   706' x 71' x 38'

VAN ENKEVORT TUG & BARGE CO.: They own a unique and newly constructed tug/barge, which is already making trips to the Twin Ports.

GREAT LAKES TRADER   TB   2000   16,000   710' x 78' x 45'

Where The Boats Are

This is where the self guided tour begins to help you see as many boats as possible in the harbor. All sites listed here are numbered in sequence, and are shown on the map on the next two pages. Your tour begins at the Duluth Aerial Bridge and piers at Canal Park, and ends at the Superior piers on Wisconsin Point. Before heading for Canal Park to start, you may want to experience the view of the city and harbor from Skyline Drive. On a clear day, the scene here is truly magnificent, and you will get a good "overview" by being able to see most of the harbor from one vantage point. To reach Skyline Drive from downtown Duluth, proceed west on Superior Street to 24th Avenue West. Turn right and follow this up the hill for about 14 blocks to Skyline, which is well signed. Turn right, and follow it for a short way to Enger Park, a well known local landmark. You can climb to the top of Enger Tower, or use the gazebo on the edge of the cliff for great views and photographs.

Before beginning our boatwatching tour, just a few words

Harbor view from Enger Park, Duluth.

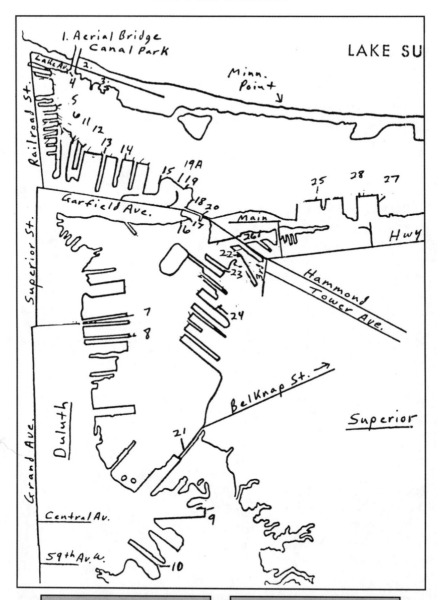

LAKE SU

1. Aerial Bridge
Canal Park
Minn.
Point

Lake Av.
Railroad St.

Garfield Ave.
Superior St.
Main
Hwy
Hammond Tower Ave.

Grand Ave.
Duluth
Belknap St.
Superior

Central Av.
59th Av. w.

LEGEND

1. Canal Park & Piers	5. Huron Cement
2. Corps of Engineers	6. Cutler Salt
3. Coast Guard	7. DM & IR Ore Dock
4. Bayfront Park	8. Hallet #5
	(See Legend Page 25)

J. A. Baumhofer

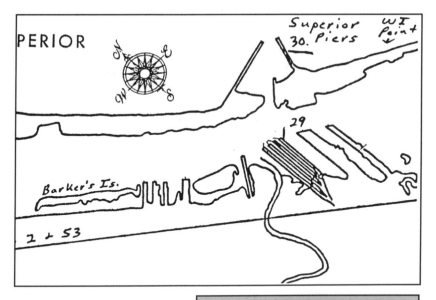

Just

Follow

The

Numbers

LEGEND	
9.	Reiss Inland Dock
10.	Hallett #6
11.	General Mills "A"
12.	Cargill
13.	Northland Dock
14.	AGP Elevator
15.	Port Terminal #1
16.	Boat Launching
17.	Interstate Bridge
18.	St. Lawrence Cement
19.	Port Terminal
19A.	Murphy Oil
20.	Blatnik High Bridge
21.	Richard Bong Bridge
22.	Harvest States
23.	General Mills "S"
24.	Midwest Energy
25.	Peavey Connor's Pt.
26.	Fraser Shipyard
27.	Cutler Stone Dock
28.	Huron Cement
29.	Burlington Northern
30.	Superior Piers

of caution. Most of the sites listed in this book are private property. Over many years of watching and photographing boats, I have never been asked to leave or had any problem visiting any of the sites. However, you should proceed with caution and consideration at all areas. Also, how we act when visiting a site could make a difference in future access. Often, a call ahead or a stop at the office to ask permission is all that is necessary. However, my inclusion of a site in this book is NOT meant to be a guarantee that it is open to the public, and this should be borne in mind while boatwatching. Also, a number of the areas listed are off the beaten path, and the streets leading to them are sometimes not in the best repair. Again, I have had few problems, and have driven to the areas in all seasons. But, it is best to drive slowly, according to the existing conditions at the time of your visit.

For a view of the harbor as seen by the boats, I recommend taking a tour on the Vista Fleet. The Vista boats give a thorough tour of both the Duluth and Superior sides of the harbor, always stopping at any areas where boats are docked. If an interesting boat is in port, they will usually stop and take extra time for viewing and photography. They have several tours daily from May to October, and can be boarded at their dock on Harbor Drive, and on Barkers Island in Superior. Also, an evening dinner cruise on the VISTA STAR can be a memorable treat.

Finally, you can begin your boatwatching day, hopefully on a bright and beautiful summer or fall morning at Canal Park. The sun is shining, gulls are circling and calling, and there is just enough breeze off the lake to give the air a fresh, cool tang. In short, it's a great day to be in the Twin Ports! You have already checked the boat listings at the Marine Museum, and there is some interesting harbor traffic. Ore boats are loading here and in Superior, a thousand footer is due for the Midwest Energy coal dock, and a couple of Canadian boats are due to arrive to load grain. There are a lot of boats to see, so let's go!

1. DULUTH PIERS, CANAL PARK, AERIAL BRIDGE.
To many boatwatchers, resident and visitor alike, the
Duluth piers at Canal Park are the prime boatwatching spot
in the area. All traffic in or out of the Duluth side of the harbor passes under the Aerial Bridge. Though all communications between the bridge and boats are now by the marine
radio, the traditional whistles still give a thrill to all boat
buffs. Canal Park's close proximity to the boats, plus the
Marine Museum and Lakewalk, make it an important first
stop. After exploring here, head south on Lake Avenue
across the Aerial Bridge. Across the bridge you reach
Minnesota Point, more commonly known as Park Point.
Park Point is really a giant sandbar formed over the centuries by wave action, which shelters the entire harbor. Lake
Avenue becomes Minnesota Avenue here.

Proceed down Minnesota Ave. to Ninth Street, where you
will find #2, the U. S. ARMY CORPS OF ENGINEERS VES-
SEL YARD. There are usually Corps of Engineers dredges
and tugs docked here. Back on Minnesota Ave., proceed to
Twelfth Street and #3, the DULUTH COAST GUARD STA-
TION. The buoy tender SUNDEW, built in Duluth in 1944,
is moored here when she is in port. You can also often see
other Coast Guard vessels. From here you can continue out
to the end of Park Point. There are frequent views of the
harbor and open lake along the way. For those of you with
other interests, Park Point has a swimming beach and hiking trails, and is one of the region's premier birding spots in
spring and fall.

Next, head back across the Aerial Bridge to Lake
Avenue, circle around, and then turn left on Harbor
Drive. You will soon see the WILLIAM A. IRVIN museum
boat, docked in the Minnesota Slip adjacent to the Duluth
Entertainment Convention Center (DECC). Also along
Harbor Drive is the Vista Fleet dock, mentioned earlier.
Follow this street as it loops around the DECC and new
Great Lakes Aquarium to #4, BAYFRONT PARK. There is
a good parking area here, and a very nice viewing area for
the inner harbor. Also there is a small playground here
for the kids.

Harbor Drive turns into Railroad Street just beyond Bayfront Park. Turn left here, and after a few blocks you will notice #5, the LAFARGE (HURON) CEMENT DOCK on your left. If any boats are unloading here, there are good views, and you can obtain excellent stern photos. Follow Railroad Street about four blocks to the turnoff for Twelfth Avenue West, and you will see #6, the CUTLER SALT DOCK. Boats are not here often, but when one is unloading salt, you can usually get a nice close view, and it is a good spot for afternoon photography.

Continue west along Railroad St. for a few blocks to Garfield Avenue. Turn right on Garfield for two blocks to Superior Street, and then left. Follow Superior Street west for a little over a mile. At this point you will notice the Duluth Missabe & Iron Range (DM & IR) railway trestle which leads to the ore docks. Keep following Superior Street here as it winds around between the freeway and Wade Stadium. After a short distance, turn left, across the freeway, and take another left to #7, the DM & IR ORE DOCKS. There is a good parking area here, and they have a nice elevated viewing platform where all

The PHILIP R. CLARKE loads taconite pellets at the DM & IR Ore Dock.

aspects of boat loading can be seen. This is by far the best viewing spot for any ore dock in the area, and the only one really open to the public. All types of lake boats, from the thousand foot super lakers to older freighters, can be seen loading here. Recently, they have installed unloading hoppers for limestone This means that a boat can unload her limestone cargo (which is then taken by rail to the taconite plants on the Iron Range) and load a taconite cargo without shifting from one dock to another. This is a great spot for photography, especially later in the day, and you can get some interesting night shots here as well.

Immediately to the west of the ore dock is #8, the HALLETT DOCK #5, used by boats to unload stone cargoes. It is possible to park near the dock office, and walk back east along the railroad tracks here for a short distance. You can then get a good view of the boats unloading, and good afternoon photos. This dock is also sometimes good in the winter, as several boats are often laid up here.

After checking DM & IR and the Hallett Dock, retrace your drive back to Superior Street. Go back east a short way to Carlton Street and turn left for two blocks to Grand Avenue. Here, you can take a side trip to visit two more of the harbor's lesser known stone docks. Turn left on Grand Avenue and proceed to Central Avenue, about one mile. Turn left on Central to Main Street for about five blocks, then left again on Main to Raleigh Street. You will soon note #9, the REISS INLAND DOCK, at Raleigh and Lesure Streets. Access is not good here, but boats can sometimes be seen unloading stone or coal. Retrace your drive back to Central Avenue and Grand. Turn left again on Grand Avenue and proceed along to 59th Avenue West. Turn left on 59th, and drive a few blocks to #10, the HALLETT DOCK #6. Though some boats do unload here, this is primarily a loading dock for petroleum coke, Bentonite clay, etc. Both lakers and salties call here. Sometimes you can drive up to the office and park there, but if the entrance is blocked by a train, it is best to park on 59th

Avenue West and walk in. You can ask at the office and get permission to walk out to view and photograph the loading. Be sure and watch your step on the slippery clay. You can also get good views of these docks from the Vista Fleet boats, and from the Richard Bong bridge, mentioned later.

Retrace your drive back to 59th Avenue West and Grand Avenue. Then, head back east on Grand Avenue and Superior Street to the intersection of Superior and Garfield Avenue. Turn right on Garfield, and the port's grain elevators will soon come into view. This is Rice's Point, where some of the earliest settlements in Duluth were located. The first elevator on your left is #11, the GENERAL MILLS ELEVATOR "A". Turn off Garfield and drive across the railroad tracks to the small parking area. This is about the best spot for grain elevator viewing, and you can get very close views and good photos. Canadian boats are seen here most often, and it is sometimes also used as a layby berth for boats waiting for another dock.

Back on Garfield, turn left for a very short distance to #12, the CARGILL ELEVATORS. The most modern in the

The ALGONORTH loads grain at General Mills Elevator "A".

port, Cargill often loads both salties and lakers. Turn left at the Cargill sign. At this point, you can either curve around to the right on the blacktop road, park, and walk across the grassy area for viewing, or drive straight in on the road that leads to the loading spouts. This is another great spot for photography. The B-1 elevator is the only one of the Cargill complex used for boat loading, while the B-2 elevator next door is sometimes used by boats to unload grain.

Back to Garfield, turn left again and drive a few blocks to Birch Avenue. Turn left here, cross the very bumpy railroad tracks, and you will see #13, the NORTHLAND BITUMINOUS CO. DOCK. This site is relatively new, and boats occasionally call here to unload stone. Next to this dock, you will note #14, the AGP GRAIN COMPANY ELEVATOR. Though a busy elevator, access is not as good here as at the previous two. You can park just before the elevator entrance and walk to the edge of the slip for views and photos.

After this, follow Birch Avenue for another short distance, as it becomes Arthur Avenue. Keeping an eye out for trains, follow this until it ends near the water. Park here, and walk out to the edge of the slip for a great view of #15, the PORT TERMINAL SLIP #1. Salties are often

Unloading general cargo at Port Terminal #1.

here unloading steel, and this is where many of the unusual imported general cargoes are unloaded by the giant cranes. Photography is good here later in the day.

Retrace your drive back to Garfield Avenue and turn left. In a few blocks you will note the turnoff for the Port Terminal. Keep right here, and it becomes Port Terminal Drive. Follow this for a block or so to #16, the BOAT LAUNCHING RAMP. You can park here, and get long distance views of boats at the Midwest Energy Terminal coal dock, the Harvest States elevators, and any traffic in or out of the DM & IR ore dock. Some good night photos can be taken here with your telephoto lens. Adjacent to the boat ramp is #17, the OLD INTERSTATE BRIDGE, one of the top boatwatching spots in Duluth. You can park in the lot, and it is an easy walk to the end of the old bridge, now a fishing pier. Here, you are on the main shipping channel, with an excellent view of most boat traffic. This is great for photography, and is especially good in summer when Canal Park is jammed with non-boatwatching tourists.

Next to the Interstate Bridge is #13, the ST. LAWRENCE CEMENT DOCK. Canadian boats call here

The CANADIAN LEADER unloads cement at the St. Lawrence Cement Dock.

fairly often to unload cement. Normally you can park near the entrance and walk in on the access road, being careful to watch for cement trucks driving in and out. Photography is very good here, and you can also drive close to the other end of this dock from the small Port Terminal road along the water's edge.

From here, continue along Port Terminal Drive to #19, the PORT TERMINAL DOCKS & BERTHING AREA. Boats of all types often tie up here to wait for dock space, or for minor repairs, inspections, etc. This is a great spot, as you can drive and walk right next to the boats, with great photo opportunities most of the day. The Port

Winter activity at the Port Terminal.

Terminal is very good in winter, as there are usually several boat laid up here for the season. Next on Port Terminal Drive you will note #19A, the MURPHY OIL COMPANY FUEL DOCK. A new harbor facility, boats are often tied up here to take on fuel, and can be easily viewed and photographed.

Returning to Garfield Avenue, turn right for a short way, then take a left for the entry ramp to I-535 and Superior. This takes you over #20, the JOHN A. BLATNIK BRIDGE, commonly called the "high bridge." There is a great overall harbor view here, but no stopping is allowed. However, boat activity can often be seen on the drive across. While discussing the subject of Twin Ports bridges, I would like to mention the other main one crossing the harbor, #21, the RICHARD I. BONG BRIDGE. Named for the legendary World War II aviator, this bridge connects 46th Avenue West and I-35 in Duluth with Belknap Street in Superior. It provides a great view of the western harbor, and has a nice walking and bike path.

Loading grain at Harvest States #2 Elevator, Superior.

Back to the main tour, head across the Blatnik High Bridge to Superior. Approaching Superior, you will pass almost directly over #22, the HARVEST STATES ELE-VATORS. Among the busiest in the harbor, a boat or two will usually be loading here. Access here can be a little difficult. Turn right off the bridge and then go straight for a block, across the main street. Then turn right, under the high bridge and across the railroad tracks. After another block, you can park and get good views from this point, which is directly across the slip from Harvest States Elevator #2. If the grain trucks that are often parked here are in the way, you may have to walk around them. Next, retrace your route for about two blocks. At this point turn right and go down the short road (Dock Street) that leads to the Harvest States office. It is normally possible to take this road right down to where the boats are loading at the Harvest States #1 and Gallery Elevators.

After this, proceed back toward Superior for a few blocks to Tower Avenue. Tower Avenue is the main street of downtown Superior, and won't be hard to locate. Follow Tower Avenue about six blocks to Winter Street. Turn right on Winter Street and in about three blocks you will note the sign for #23, the GENERAL MILLS "S" ELEVATOR. Turn right down the somewhat rough access road. This is the old Great Northern Elevator, an historic harbor landmark, and once the largest grain elevator on the Great Lakes. These days, it is used only occasionally, but when a boat is at the dock it's a good spot for photography.

Retrace your drive back to Winter Street and turn right. After a short distance you will come to #24, the MIDWEST ENERGY RESOURCES CO. coal terminal. Not really open to the public, you can often just drive in

The ARTHUR M. ANDERSON loads coal at the Midwest Energy Terminal, Superior.

on the access road and park at the employee lot. From here, it is possible to get nice stern photos of any boat that may be loading. Next, retrace your route back to the corner of Winter Street and Tower Avenue. Turn left on Tower, back toward the waterfront, and follow Hwy. 2 and 53 to the right. This is a busy highway, so stay in the left lane for about seven blocks, to the sign for Main Street. Turn left here, and follow it across the railroad tracks. This is Connor's Point, one of the oldest sections of Superior. Turn left, and you will note two important harbor facilities. The first is #25, the PEAVEY CONNOR'S POINT ELEVATOR. Boats are often loading here, and you can drive in on the access road for great views and photography.

Back on Main Street, you will be directly across from #26, the FRASER SHIPYARD. This is the site of Alexander McDougall's original shipyard where many of the whaleback steamers (like the METEOR) were built. It was also important to national defense during World War II. Unfortunately, Fraser is one of the few boatwatching sites strictly off limits to visitors. Luckily, however, it is possible to see almost as much from Main Street as in the yard itself. Just park anywhere along the way, and walk through the weeds down to the edge of the slip. Again, winter is one of the best times here. Several boats are normally laid up, and you can often get good views of ongoing repairs in the drydock.

On the right side off of Main Street, you will probably note the JOHN SHERWIN. Inactive for many years, she and other inactive Interlake boats are often berthed here. Boatwatchers are hoping the rumors that she will be converted to a self-unloader and put back in use will come true. Main Street comes to a dead end at the end of Connor's Point. Here, you can park, and walk to the end of the point for some nice harbor views.

Next, return to the main highway. Turn left here for about one-half mile to the next left. Turn off here and curve around, and soon #27, the CUTLER STONE DOCK can be seen. Lakers are sometimes here unloading stone, and you can get a good view and photos by waking down close to the slip. Proceed another short distance on this road to #29, the LAFARGE (HURON) CEMENT DOCK. Drive in on the access road and park. Inland Lakes cement carriers usually unload part of their cargo here, and part at their dock in Duluth. This dock is the better of the two for photography. Also, the very historic steamer J. B. FORD, built in 1904, is moored here, and used for cement storage.

The J. B. FORD, now docked at Lafarge Cement Dock, Superior.

Return to the main highway, and turn left again. You will soon pass Barker's Island on the harbor side. This makes an interesting detour, as it is home to the museum boat METEOR, the old dredge D. D. GAILLARD, and other nautical attractions.

Continue east on the main highway for about two and one-half miles to 39th Avenue East. Turn left here for one block to Itasca Street, and then right for another block to 40th Avenue East. Take another left here to the entrance to #29, the BURLINGTON NORTHERN SANTA FE ORE DOCK. After going through the gate, take the first left,

Loading taconite pellets at the Burlington Northern Ore dock, Superior.

and drive along the access road for a few blocks. This gives a great view of boats at the dock. You can also drive straight ahead down to the dock itself. It is best to ask permission for this, and be prepared to have yourself and your car covered with the reddish ore dust. This is a great photo spot, except very early in the day.

Next, return to the main highway, and turn left again. Proceed for about two miles to the turnoff for #30, the SUPERIOR PIERS AND SHIP CANAL. There should be

Foreign ship arriving at the Superior piers.

a sign here for Lake Superior and Wisconsin Point. Turn left here, then left again on the Wisconsin Point Road. This is a very scenic drive, with great opportunities to view birds and other wildlife, the historic Indian burial grounds, and the Wisconsin Point lighthouse. You'll be amazed at how few people there are here than at Minnesota Point in Duluth.

After about three miles, the road ends at the Superior piers. This is an important area to check, as there are some boats, such as the STEWART J. CORT and GEORGE A. STINSON that use the Superior entrance almost exclusively, on their way to load at B. N. Every boat coming in to load at the ore dock, and most coming to load at the Peavey Connor's Point elevator, uses this harbor entrance.

This concludes the Twin Ports portion of our boat-watching tour. It should be obvious by now that it may be difficult to manage the entire tour in one day. Particularly if some of the side trips are taken, it's probably best to spread your tour out over more than one day. One big advantage in having more than one day is that the boat situation often changes very quickly. One day may be poor, with few boats around, and the next day the harbor can be bustling with traffic.

Having said this, I also realize that the Twin Ports are a very popular one-day or weekend destination. Not everyone will have several days at their disposal to take the entire tour. With this in mind, I have singled out the top seven boatwatching sites, for an easy one day tour. By far, the best and most interesting stops to make are: #1, CANAL PARK & THE DULUTH PIERS; #4, the BAYFRONT PARK; #7, THE DM & IR DULUTH ORE DOCK; #17, the INTERSTATE BRIDGE; #19, the PORT TERMINAL; #22, the HARVEST STATES ELEVATORS; and #30, WISCONSIN POINT & THE SUPERIOR PIERS. By just checking these sites, it will be quite possible to see a good variety of boats in a short time.

After your Twin Ports tour, you may wish to check out the boat activity on the North Shore. Two Harbors, about

The EDGAR B. SPEER and PRESQUE ISLE loading at the DM & IR Ore Dock, Two Harbors.

25 miles northeast of Duluth on scenic Highway 61, is the most significant. The DM & IR ore docks at Two Harbors are very busy, and it is usually possible to see an interesting boat. Just follow the signs for the waterfront,

Historic tug EDNA G and Two Harbors ore dock.

about one-half mile to the right off the highway. The historic tugboat EDNA G is moored on the waterfront next to the ore dock. Listed on the National Register of Historic Places, the EDNA G was one of the last coal-fired tugs to operate on the lakes, and was built in 1896. She is open for daily tours in the summer, and is fascinating to visit. Other Two Harbors attractions include the interesting Lake County Historical Museum in the old depot. This features many wonderful displays, along with two historic locomotives.

About 30 miles up the North Shore, you will reach Silver Bay. Northshore Mining Company recently reactivated the old Reserve Mining Co. plant here to process taconite pellets. Viewing here isn't too good, but you can check out some of the activity from the small park south of town. The last boatwatching stop on the North Shore is Taconite Harbor, about 25 miles beyond Silver Bay. The ore dock here is built in a manmade harbor at the mouth of the Two Island River. Sadly, the LTV operations at Taconite Harbor were closed in 2001. A few boats may still be delivering coal to the power plant near the dock, but its future is very uncertain. To check for possible boat activity, turn right off the highway just before the railroad bridge. The somewhat rough road winds down to the lake, where the ore dock can be seen.

After checking Taconite Harbor, it is only about 80 miles to the Canadian border, and then a short 40 mile drive to Thunder Bay. This drive is one of the most scenic in the country. There is nothing more in the way of shipping, but there are several great attractions. I recommend at least stopping at Grand Marais and Grand Portage.

Just north of Grand Portage are two roadside rest areas with spectacular views of the lake and surrounding mountainous shoreline. On clear days, Isle Royale can be glimpsed near the horizon. After this, it is only a few miles to the Canadian border at the Pigeon River. After entering Ontario, the road (still Highway 61) curves away from Lake Superior for the drive into Thunder Bay. Along the way, you will note the ruggedly beautiful Nor'Wester Mountains, named for the early Northwest Company, with its fur traders and explorers.

The Canadian Lakehead

What is now Thunder Bay began as two cities with very distinct personalities. The south half was originally Fort William, and the north half Port Arthur. They maintained a unique (and sometimes quarrelsome) relationship for many decades, before a government-mandated merger in 1970. After this, the "new" city of Thunder Bay has become a strong industrial port city, with quite rapid growth.

Thunder Bay is a fascinating place to visit. One of the first things to strike American visitors is the cultural diversity of the city. Boasting the world's largest Finnish population outside Finland, Thunder Bay is also home to many Ukrainians, Italians, and many other nationalities. Often, these groups have kept their own neighborhoods and shopping areas. Thus, in many parts of the city, it is easy to get the feel of being in Europe, and there are great opportunities for shopping, sampling ethnic foods, etc.

The story of the port of Thunder Bay really comes down to one word: grain. What the iron ore of Minnesota meant to Duluth-Superior, the golden wheat of the Canadian prairies meant to Port Arthur and Fort William. Grain has been shipped down the lakes from Thunder Bay for over 100 years. The first shipments were of bagged wheat that had been stored in sheds, before the port's elevators were even built. The port shipped its first wheat cargo on the Str. ERIN in the fall of 1883. The following year saw construction of the first small grain elevator, and by 1886, the port had already reached a volume of three million bushels.

Today, Thunder Bay has the world's largest concentration of grain elevators, with total storage capacity of over 85 million bushels. In the record year of 1983, the port shipped over 17 million tons of grain! That same year, an amazing 9,672 railcars of grain were received, graded and unloaded in one seven-day period. Since then, changes in the pattern of grain shipments from the St. Lawrence Seaway to the west coast of Canada have lowered grain totals. However, though times have changed and the port has diversified, grain is still king. Normally, the port still ships over ten million tons of grain yearly.

Thunder Bay handles several other important cargoes. Large quantities of western coal and potash are shipped from two bulk terminals. Also, liquid bulk cargoes of petroleum and chemical products are more important here than in the Twin Ports. Thunder Bay also handles many general cargoes from the Keefer Terminal. As in Duluth, these labor intensive cargoes have been on the rise here. Lumber and other forest products are another important cargo.

Boatwatching in Thunder Bay is quite different from the Twin Ports. The lake, harbor and aerial bridge seem to dominate Duluth. By contrast, in Thunder Bay it is sometimes difficult to even realize you are in a port city. This lack of access to and visibility of the boats is most noticeable in the southern part of town. In the north half, city streets climb the hills (as in Duluth) and the waterfront is visible from most points, the horizon framed by the Sleeping Giant. This impressive formation, actually part of the Sibley Peninsula, is probably Thunder Bay's most well known landmark.

As in the Twin Ports, you should get a city map and other tourist information at a visitor center before

View of Thunder Bay harbour from Hillcrest Park.

starting to explore. Then, as a first stop, I suggest visiting Hillcrest Park, on High Street off of Red River Road. This is a great spot to get an overall view of most of the harbour. You can often see boat traffic from here, and there is a good view of many of the huge grain elevators. In summer, the park features beautiful flower gardens.

THE SLEEPING GIANT

There are some interesting legends and lore surrounding many of the Lakehead landmarks. One of the best known Indian legends tells the story of the Sleeping Giant. Centuries ago, Nanabijou, a giant and one of the Ojibway gods, walked the land. He protected the Ojibway, and guarded the rich underwater silver deposits at Silver Islet. Only the Ojibway knew the secret of this vast silver hoard, and the secret was kept due to the warning of Nanabijou: if the white man ever discovered this treasure, the Indians would die, and he himself would be turned to stone.

One day, a Sioux scout from the south heard Nanabijou's warning, and hurried off to tell his tribe.

The Sleeping Giant.

On the way, he came across two white traders to whom he told the secret of the great Silver Islet mine. As they neared the island, a terrific storm broke over the lake. Lightning flashed, and huge waves swamped the canoes carrying the traders and the scout. The storm finally subsided, and a giant rock formation had risen from the waters of Thunder Bay. It was the form of a sleeping giant, his arms folded across his chest! The secret of the silver mine had been revealed, and Nanabijou no longer protected the Ojibway. Millions of dollars worth of silver were extracted from the mine at Silver Islet, which operated from 1869 to 1884.

The only drawback to Thunder Bay boatwatching is that access to port facilities is more limited than in the Twin Ports. It often takes more work to find the boats here. Once you do, however, it is well worth the effort. Also, the same precautions regarding asking permission and respecting private property rights apply here as in the Twin Ports. Again, if you call ahead and explain your reasons for wanting to see and photograph boats, access is often no problem.

Our Thunder Bay tour is laid out in one long loop, the same as the Twin Ports. The tour loop starts and ends at Prince Arthur Park and marina, on the waterfront below Hillcrest Park. Here again, it is probably better to split the tour into two or more segments, to be done on different days if time permits. Thunder Bay's phone number for boat information is (807) 345-1256. Updated frequently throughout the day, this number lists all boats in port and their locations. It does not list expected arrivals, however, so it is best to call every few hours for updates.

So, after calling the boat update line and stopping at Hillcrest Park, continue down to the waterfront on Red River Road, to Prince Arthur Park and marina. From here, drive back one block to Cumberland Street. Turn right on Cumberland for about three blocks to the Graham Street overpass. Turn right again, and as you

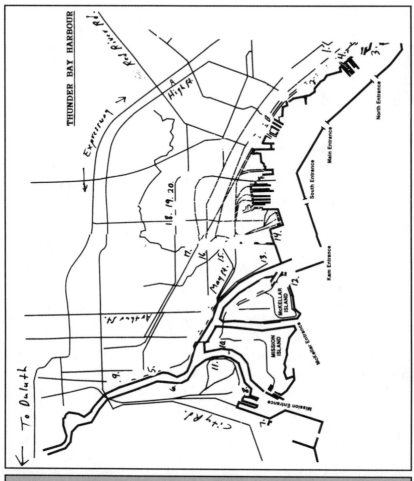

A. Hillcrest Park
B. Prince Arthur Park
1. Richardson Elevator
2. Great West Timber
3. PASCOL Engineering
4. United Grain Gro. "A"
5. Western Grain By-Prod.
6. General Chemical
7. Cargill Elevator
8. Mission Terminal
9. (Changing hands)
10. Petro Canada
11. Valley Camp
12. Thunder Bay Terminal
13. Imperial Oil
14. Keefer Terminal
15. United Grain Gro. "M"
16. Agricore Elevator
17. P & H Elevator
18. Sask. Pool 7A
19. Sask. Pool 7B
20. Canada Malting

Loading grain at the Richardson Elevator.

follow the overpass, it becomes Water Street. Turn left here, and proceed 1.2 miles to #1, the RICHARDSON ELEVATOR. Along the way, you will pass #2, the GREAT WEST TIMBER DOCK. Tugs occasionally call here to pick up lifts of lumber. The Richardson elevator is an excellent viewing spot, and there is usually a boat here. The elevator's bright orange-red color was long one of the harbour's well known features. However, it is in the process of being re-painted blue and white at press time.

Next, retrace your route back to Graham and Cumberland Street. From here, proceed 1.8 miles on Cumberland to Grenville Avenue. Turn right on Grenville to #3, PASCOL ENGINEERING, on Shipyard Road. This is the former Port Arthur Shipyard, an historic part of the harbour. Boats are often in here for repair, and winter layup. The best way to see them is to turn left at the shipyard entrance, and park about a block ahead. You can then walk up the embankment across the road for a fairly good view of the yard. Then go back on Shipyard Road and turn left on the first blacktop, known as Fisherman's Road. This leads down to a small boat landing. Here, you can walk out on the

United Grain Growers Elevator "A".

dock for a great view of #4, the UNITED GRAIN GROW-
ER'S ELEVATOR "A". Boats are often loading here, and
it is a good spot for early and midday photos. You can
also get another look at the shipyard here. Returning to
Shipyard Road, turn left and drive past United Grain
Growers "A". At this point, you can get nice bow photos
of boats at this dock. Next, retrace your route back to
Grenville and Cumberland. Turn right on Cumberland,
and it soon turns into Hodder Avenue. Follow Hodder
Avnue for about two miles to the Thunder Bay
Expressway, Highways 11-17. Turn left on the expressway, and take this back several miles to the south end of
town. At the Airport intersection, keep going straight
ahead, following the signs for Highway 61. Follow Hwy.
61 across the Kaministiquia River (known locally as the
"Kam") to Highway 61B, the City Road.

Turn left on City Road. After reaching the turnoff
where 61B crosses the Kam River back into town, continue on City Road for another mile, to the sign for the
McAsphalt Co. By turning in here and asking permission, you can get a view of #5, the WESTERN GRAIN
BY-PRODUCTS DOCK, across the river. Sometimes a
saltie will be loading here. Returning to the City Road,
turn left here for a short distance to #6, the GENERAL
CHEMICAL DOCK. Tankers occasionally call here to
off-load cargoes of liquid calcium chloride.

Retrace your route back to City Rd., and turn left for another short way. Soon you will see the sign for Cargill. After the sign, take the second left, which leads to #7, the CAR-GILL ELEVA-TOR, and #8, the MISSION TERMINAL ELEVATOR. Follow the access road to Cargill, which has a parking area, and a good viewing

Loading grain at the Cargill Elevator.

and photographic spot. Take the other fork in the access road for the Mission Terminal. Formerly Saskatchewan Pool #15, this elevator has been re-activated recently, and hopefully will again be a good viewing spot.

After this, continue on James St. for two blocks to Gore Street. Turn right on Gore and, after five blocks, Gore turns into Ford Street. Turn left on Ford and go three blocks to Brock Street, and turn right. Follow Brock for three blocks until it turns into Syndicate Avenue. Follow Syndicate for about six blocks, and you will note New Vickers Street and the old jackknife bridge on the right. On your right at this point is #10, the PETRO CANADA DOCK. Tankers from several fleets are often here, but access is difficult.

Continue on this road, which becomes 106th Street,

for about one mile, to 108th Avenue. Turn right here on the road to the Thunder Bay Generating Station. Before the plant, you can see if a boat is at #11, the VALLEY CAMP DOCK, across the Mission River from here. Both lakers and salties often load at Valley Camp. You can park near the power plant entrance, and walk down to the river bank. This can be a good spot for morning and midday photos with your telephoto lens.

Retrace your route back to 106th Street, and turn left for a short distance to 104th Avenue. Turn right, and cross another old drawbridge to McKellar Island. After about two miles, you will note #12, the THUNDER BAY TERMINALS. The road ends here, and access is not very good. However, it may be possible to arrange for a tour by calling them in advance. Thunder Bay terminals is similar to Midwest Energy in Superior, and ships mainly western Canadian coal and potash. At this point, you can also get a view of #13, the IMPERIAL OIL DOCK, across the Kam River. If a tanker is at the dock, you can park at the Thunder Bay Terminal entrance, and walk through the brush on an old access road to the river bank. You will need a long telephoto lens for any success at photography. Retrace your drive back to Syndicate Avenue, across the jackknife bridge. Turn right on Syndicate for four blocks to Arthur Street. Turn right on Arthur for two blocks, and then turn left on May Street. Proceed .for about two miles on May Street, as it becomes Memorial Avenue. Soon you will be in the heart of Thunder Bay harbour.

At the Intercity Mall on Memorial Avenue, turn right on Main Street. This leads to #14, the KEEFER TERMINAL, the port's general cargo facility. Though not open to the public, you can often get permission to view the boats by calling their office. Before the terminal entrance, turn left on Hammond Avenue for a short distance to Maureen Street. Turn right for about a block here, and you will pass on your left #15, the UNITED GRAIN GROWERS "M" ELEVATOR; #16, the AGRICORE ELEVATOR; and #17, the P & H GRAIN COMPANY ELEVATOR. Boats are often loading at any or all of these, depending on the season. You can normally park in the lots for good views.

Next, turn around and go back on Maureen Street. A short distance ahead, you will soon see #18, the SASKATCHEWAN POOL #7A ELEVATOR. The parking lot here is one of the best viewing spots in the harbour, with great photo opportunities. Next, you will see (in order), #19, the SASKATCHEWAN POOL #7B ELEVATOR; and #20, the CANADA MALTING C0. ELEVA-

Waiting to load at Saskatchewan Pool 7A.

TOR. The access is not as good here as at Pool 7A, but all of them should be check for boat activity.

After this, turn left on Central Avenue, back to Fort William Road. Turn right here for about two miles as it becomes Water Street. This will return you to Prince Arthur Park and Marina, the tour ending point.

As in the Twin Ports, there are many great tourist spots in Thunder Bay. Again, I won't attempt to detail them here, and you can refer to the readily available visitor guides. Kakabeka Falls (the Niagara of the North), the accurately restored old Fort William, Mount McKay, Ouimet Canyon, and the city's many parks and gardens are all worth a stop.

If you have an extra day for sightseeing, one side

trip is really rewarding. Take Highway 11-17 east out of town. Though traffic can be heavy, the scenery is great. About 59 miles from Thunder Bay, you can turn right on Hwy. 628 for a few miles to the town of Red Rock. Home to large paper and pulp mills, Red Rock was formerly an important harbor for lake boats carrying newsprint to cities in the lower Great Lakes. The fast package freighters of Canada Steamship Lines often called here in years past. Now there is a scenic park on the water-front, with a golf course and boat landing, and great views of the high bluffs surrounding the town.

Returning to the main highway, turn right for another eight miles to the town of Nipigon. Famous for trophy fish, Nipigon has a marina and interesting historical museum. Just east of town, the highway crosses the Nipigon River, the largest tributary of Lake Superior. After this, turn left on Highway 11. Soon you will note Lake Helen, part of the Nipigon River and a large, beautiful lake completely framed by high rock walls.

Near the Lake Helen Indian Reserve, you will see St. Sylvester's Church on your right. One of the oldest structures in the region, it was built in 1877 by early missionaries. Be sure to stop here, as the church and adjacent old cemetery overlooking Lake Helen are very picturesque.

Historic St. Sylvester's Church, Lake Helen.

Keep following Hwy. 11 as it winds through almost mountainous country. During rainy weather there are many small waterfalls on the high cliffs.

After several miles of this great scenery, you will reach Orient Bay, and your first view of Lake Nipigon. Next come Macdiarmid and the Rocky Bay Indian Reserve, both interesting old villages. After another 20 miles you will come to the small town of Beardmore. Note the town mascot the "Beardmore Snowman" on your right as you arrive. By now, it's not hard to get the feeling of being in the "real" north country. Turn left on Highway 580 here for the short four mile drive to the shore of Lake Nipigon.

Regarded as the sixth Great Lake by many, Lake Nipigon is little publicized and even less often visited. Its huge size alone make it awesome to contemplate. Measuring over 65 miles long (north to south) and 40 miles wide, Lake Nipigon has 580 miles of shoreline and over 1000 islands! With maximum depths of over 500 feet, it is the northernmost watershed of the entire Great Lakes system. Of the islands, 55 are over 64 acres in size, and there are 35 interior lakes on four of the largest islands. These islands are one of the farthest south in North America that the rare Woodland Caribou can be seen. Of course, the entire area is a paradise for fishing, hiking and wildlife viewing. The sight of the landless horizon of Lake Nipigon, set in this true northern wilderness, is really unforgettable. After this, Thunder Bay and Duluth seem like the big city!

BEHIND THE SCENES

In this chapter I will try to give you a feel for some of the things that happen every day with the boats, but are little known to most observers. One of the most important "behind the scenes" activities is radio communications. Every time a boat enters or leaves the harbor, ties up to or departs from a dock, or moves anywhere, its intentions must be broadcast over the marine radio. Known as a "security call," it announces the boat's intended movements, including arrival and departure times. This is done to alert any other boat traffic in the harbor. If other boats are in the area, they will answer the boat making the security call. Then, the two captains will decide what course to take, where to pass each other, etc. The radio has many other uses as well, including notifying the Duluth Aerial Bridge that a boat is arriving, talking with the docks, receiving weather reports, etc.

Each fleet of lakers and foreign ships arriving in port has a local agent. The agents arrange for dock space, transmit reports on cargo tonnage and other data from the boat to the fleet office, and perform many other services. On duty 24 hours daily in the shipping season, agents make sure that each boat's stop in port goes as smoothly as possible.

Also crucial to harbor operations are the tug boats. Tugs are an integral part of the day-to-day life of both harbors, and serve many purposes. Lake boats are much less dependent on tugs than they formerly were. The majority of modern lakers have bow thrusters, a steering device under the water line of the bow which enables them to maneuver in the narrow harbor chan-

Tug assisting boat into Fraser Shipyard.

nels. Before these bow thrusters were common, lake boats often needed tugs to move anywhere in the harbor. Now, tugs are used only occasionally by lakers. Entering or leaving certain docks in windy conditions, going in or out of the shipyards, or if they are having mechanical problems, are reasons why lakers may still use tugs. Also, tugs do a lot of icebreaking near most of the docks early and late in the season. All in all, tugboats are fun to watch as they hurry across the harbor, and they contribute a lot to the maritime flavor of the waterfront.

BOATWATCHING TOOLS

Like most other hobbies, there are a few tools that can make boatwatching more fun and rewarding. First on your list should be a pair of binoculars. These will come in handy for scanning the horizon for incoming boats, checking activity at the docks, etc.

Next, and probably the most important, is a scanner. If you are an avid boat fan, once you use a scanner, you'll never know how you got along without it! Scanners enable you to listen to all conversations made over the marine radio. Boat captains talking to each other, to docks and elevators, to the Aerial Bridge, the Coast Guard, tugs, and much more can all be heard. Scanners come in a wide variety of types and price ranges. Probably the best are the hand-held models, that you can take along on your boatwatching tour. To help in programming your scanner, all channels normally used by the boats are listed at the end of the book. The greatest advantage of using a scanner in boatwatching is that you will know in advance all arrival and departure times, where each boat is going, cargoes they are carrying, etc.

Last but not least among your "tools" should be a camera. Almost all boatwatchers like to take boat pictures, and you can get passable results with almost any camera. However, there are certain things you can do and buy to make your boat pictures better.

As a long time photographer, I have learned a few

tips through the years. Most people use a standard 35 mm single lens reflex camera, and these work great. Many good shots can be taken with your 35 mm camera using the standard 50 mm or 55 mm lens. However, to get the most out of your photography, you will probably want to add to these. Probably the best choice will be a zoom lens in the 28-200 mm range. This will combine wide angle and telephoto uses in a single lens. As you advance in boat photography, you will probably want to try a longer telephoto lens in the 300 mm range. This will help greatly for distance shots.

As for accessories, the most important is a polarizing filter. This does a great job of enhancing sky and water colors, and eliminating much of the glare that is common near the water on sunny days. A monopod is useful for low light conditions or strong winds, and, of course, a good tripod is a must for night shots. Night photos of boats at a dock can be some of the most interesting and dramatic you will take. For best results, use fast (400 ASA or greater) film, and bracket your exposures, using different exposure times on several different shots. Have fun with your boat pictures, and you'll probably end up with a great collection.

F Y I

In this last section, I will list some organizations you may wish to join, and local shops that handle boat-related items. First, a great organization to join is the Lake Superior Marine Museum Association, Box 177, Duluth, MN 55801. They help operate the Canal Park Marine Museum, hold frequent meetings and programs, and publish the fine newsletter THE NOR'EASTER. In my opinion, the NOR'EASTER alone is well worth the membership cost.

Also essential to the avid boat fan is the bi-weekly newsletter *GREAT LAKES SEAWAY LOG*, published by Harbor House at 221 Water St., Boyne City, MI 49712. The *LOG* is a combination news magazine and gossip column for the boats. It gives all the latest details on boat movements, industry news, unusual cargoes, interesting sightings, etc., most of which are reported by average boatwatchers from around the lakes. Cost of a subscription is $32 annually.

Along with the Boatwatcher's Hotline and the Thunder Bay boat information line already mentioned, there are some other phone numbers you can call for recorded messages about boat traffic. The DM & IR Railroad has an update line for boats at their Duluth and Two Harbors docks, (218) 628-4590. The Burlington Northern Superior ore dock has a number which is updated irregularly, (715) 394-1350. Midwest Energy Resources updates arrivals at their dock at (715) 395-3559. USS Great Lakes Fleet has a recording at (218) 628-4389, and the Oglebay Norton fleet's number is (800) 861-8760. Another line that may be of interest is the Superior chapter of the International Longshoreman's Union (ILA). They load most of the grain cargoes at the Superior elevators, and have an update line at (715) 392-1290.

There are two locally owned bookstores that carry a nice variety of nautical and regional interest books. In Duluth, try the Northern Lights Books & Gifts at 307 Canal Park Drive, and in Superior try J. W. Beecroft Books & Coffee at 3631 Tower Ave. Also, the Vista Fleet has a nice gift shop across from their dock, featuring nautical gifts and souvenirs. Lastly, there is a very informative guide to all the salties you will see on your trips. *SALTIES 2002* can be ordered from Norman Eakins at Box 595792 Fort Gratiot, MI 48059. At press time, the price was $10 U. S. postpaid. Contact Norman regarding Canadian orders.

The Top Ten

One new feature this year is my list of the ten most watchable lake boats. This very subjective listing is of boats that are often noted either for their age, beauty, uniqueness or historical significance. As you look for them, try coming up with your own "top ten."

1. ARTHUR M. ANDERSON. Typical of a formerly large group of boats built during the post World War II economic boom of the 1950s, the ANDERSON is often seen in the Twin Ports. She seems to characterize what people like about the lakers. Of course, she is also famous for being the last boat to have contact with the EDMUND FITZGERALD before the "Fitz" sank in Whitefish Bay 10 November, 1975.

2. CSL LAURENTIEN. She represents a new generation of lake boats being rebuilt by Canada Steamship Lines at the Collingwood Shipyard. They have added new forward sec-

tions and self unloading equipment to some of their older boats, greatly increasing their size and cargo capacity. In fact, they are now the largest boats able to transit the St. Lawrence Seaway. The old J. W. McGIFFIN became CSL NIAGARA, H. M. GRIFFITH became RIGHT HON. PAUL J. MARTIN, and LOUIS R.DESMARAIS is the newest addition, CSL LAURENTIEN.

3. STEWART J. CORT. A new era in Great Lakes shipping began in 1972, when the unique STEWART J. CORT made her maiden voyage. The first thousand foot bulk carrier, her bow and stern sections were built on the Gulf of Mexico, and joined to the 816 foot cargo section built in Erie, PA. The only thousand footer with a forward pilot house, the CORT proudly keeps "#1" painted near her smokestacks. Incidentally, the first thousand footer built entirely on the Great Lakes was JAMES R. BARKER.

4. J.A.W. IGLEHART. Built as a tanker in 1936, the IGLE-

HART is one of the best known of the old Huron Cement (now Lafarge) fleet. As more and more of their oldest boats are now being used only for storage, the IGLEHART and ALPENA are always greeted with interest around the lakes.

5. KINSMAN INDEPENDENT. The only U.S. flag straight deck bulk carrier now operating, the Kinsman is always sought after by boatwatchers. The third boat to carry this proud name, she was originally part of the old Hutchinson fleet, then the ERNEST R. BREECH of Ford Motor Co. She made her first Twin Ports visit as the KINSMAN in 1988, and still calls frequently for grain.

6. MIDDLETOWN. The history of this interesting old boat would almost make a book in itself! When you look at her distinctive shape, it's not too hard to see that she was built as an oceangoing tanker. She entered service for the Navy as the oiler USS NESHANIC in 1942. Seeing action in the Pacific in World War II, she was attacked by Japanese aircraft off Saipan in 1944. She survived the attack with extensive damage, but was rebuilt. After the war, as the tanker GULFOIL, she exploded in a collision with another tanker in the Atlantic in 1958, with 17 crewmen being killed. After this, she was completely rebuilt, and came to the Great Lakes as a bulk carrier in 1961. The next time you see her peacefully loading ore at Duluth or Silver Bay, take a minute to reflect on her long and turbulent life.

7. PATERSON. The last boat to be built on the Great Lakes, the PATERSON made her maiden voyage in 1985. Until the recently rebuilt CSL boats came on the scene (see above), she was also the largest boat on the Seaway, and held many grain cargo records. Early in 2002, this historic boat was renamed PINEGLEN, and now sails for Canada Steamship Lines.

8. SEAWAY QUEEN. Typifying the optimism in both the U.S. and Canada that came with the opening of the St. Lawrence Seaway in 1959, the SEAWAY QUEEN was launched the same year. For a short time she was the largest boat on the lakes, and was indeed "Queen" of the Seaway. This handsome boat hasn't been seen at the Head of the Lakes for awhile, but hopefully this will change.

9. WILFRED SYKES. This great boat was an awesome sight when she was launched in 1950. She was an engineering marvel, featuring design innovations not found on any other

boat at the time. On her first visit to Duluth in May, 1950, literally thousands of people lined up for tours. Lucky boat-watchers can still see her today on one of her all too infrequent visits.

10. PAUL R. TREGURTHA. Launched as the WILLIAM J. DeLANCEY in 1981, she and the COLUMBIA STAR are the last U.S. flag lake boats to be built. At 1,013 feet, 6 inches in length, the mighty "Paul R" is the largest boat to ever sail the Great Lakes. You can normally see (and hear!) her almost every week at the Duluth piers.

Programming Your Scanner

Most scanners now are programmable, though some use crystals. For these, you will have to buy a crystal for each frequency desired. Listed below are the frequencies most often used in the Twin Ports.

1. Channel 16, 156.800 Megahertz (Mhz), is the most important channel. It is used by all boats in making security calls, and in calling other boats and the Aerial Bridge. Once contact is made on this channel, the captains will agree to move to another frequency, as channel 16 is for calling and distress only.

2. Channel 10, 156.500 Mhz, is used to talk with the Aerial Bridge, loading dock and other boats.

3. Channel 18, 156.900 Mhz, is of interest in that it is the one normally used by the Duluth harbor tugs.

4. Channel 22, 157.100 Mhz, is used by the Duluth Coast Guard.

5. The following channels are the most often used to talk with other boats, loading docks, etc.

Channel 6: 156.300 Mhz
Channel 8: 156.400 Mhz
Channel 12: 156.600 Mhz
Channel 14: 156.700 Mhz

These channels are the most commonly heard, but there are several others. Many scanners have "search" modes where you can scan the marine band for any other frequencies a boat may be using.

J. A. Baumhofer

Boatwatchers' Phone Directory

TWIN PORTS

AGP Grain Co.	(218) 722-0538
Aerial Bridge	(218) 723-3387
B.N. Ore Dock	(715) 394-1331
Cargill Elevators	(218) 727-7219
Cutler Salt Dock	(218) 722-3981
Cutler Stone Dock	(715) 392-5146
DM & IR Ore Dock	(218) 723-2171
Fraser Shipyard	(715) 394-7787
General Mills El. "A"	(218) 722-7759
General Mills El. "S"	(715) 392-4462
Hallet Dock #.5	(218) 628-2281
Hallett Dock #6	(218) 624-0161.
Harvest States Elevator	(715 392-4734
Lafarge Cement Duluth	(218) 727-2493
Lafarge Cement Superior	(715) 392-6284
Midwest Energy Terminal	(715) 392-9807
Peavey Connor's Point El.	(715) 392-9853
Port Authority	(218) 727-8525
Reiss Inland Dock	(218) 628-2371
St. Lawrence Cement	(218) 726-1371
Vista Fleet	(218) 722-6218

THUNDER BAY
(All 807 A.C.)

Agricore Elevator	345-7351
Canada Malting Co.	344-6460
Cargill Elevator	623-6724
General Chemical Dock	622-4346
Great West Timber	343-6455
Imperial Oil Dock	623-1551
Keefer Terminal	345-6400
Mission Terminal El.	623-8868
N.M. Paterson & Sons	577-8421
P & H Elevator	345-5822
Pascol Engineering	683-6261
Petro Canada Dock	622-8701
Richardson Elevator	343-5575
Saskatchewan Pool #7	346-3351
Thunder Bay Terminals	625-7800
United Grain Growers "A"	345-4425
United Grain Growers "M"	345-8211
Valley Camp Dock	622-6463
Western Grain By-Prod.	623-8500

DULUTH HOTLINE (218) 722-6489

THUNDER BAY HARBOUR (807) 345-1256

DM & IR: (218) 628-4590

Midwest Energy: (715) 395-3559

Great Lakes Facts

While **thunderstorms** *can develop in any month, they are mostly likely from May through October.*

* * *

Fog *can form in any season, but it is most likely in spring and early summer, particularly over open waters. Oc-casionally steam fog will develop in the winter.*

* * *

High humidity *and* **temperature extremes** *that can be encountered when navigating the Great Lakes may cause sweat damage to cargo. This problem is most likely when cargoes are loaded in warm summer air or can occur any time temperatures fluctuate rapidly.*

* * *

Ice *normally begins to form in various parts of the Great Lakes during December and forms a hazard to navigation by the end of the month. Before the St. Lawrence Seaway closes in late December, most lake vessels lay up for the winter and oceangoing vessels transit the Seaway to the Atlantic.*

* * *

Lake Superior is the largest body of fresh water in the world. *Its water surface is 31,200 square miles. Next is Lake Huron with 23,000, Michigan with 22,450, Erie with 9,960, and Ontario with 7,240.*

* * *

Lake Superior is **602 feet above sea level***. The others are: Michigan at 581 ft., Huron at 581, Erie at 573, and Ontario at 247.*

* * *

In the Great Lakes bulk trade, the 2,240-pound long ton is used rather than the commercial avoirdupois ton of 2,000 pounds.

* * *

The first lighthouse on the Great Lakes built in the United States was at Buffalo, N.Y., in 1818.

J. A. Baumhofer

Did You Know?

In 1679, La Salle sailed on Lake Ontario, thus making the first recorded voyage on any of the Great Lakes.

* * *

The sloops OSWEGO and ONTARIO reportedly were the first British vessels constructed on the Great Lakes (1755).

* * *

*According to the National Oceanic and Atmospheric Administration, the Great Lakes lie in the midst of **a climatological battlefield**, where northern polar air often sturggles for control with air from the Tropics. During spring and autumn, the zone separating these two armies lies over the Lakes region. The contrast between the two triggers the formation of a number of low-pressure systems, often intense, often fast moving. These are referred to as "extratropical cyclones." The Lakes provide moisture and, in the fall, heat to fuel these winter-type storms. They also aid storms that migrate from other regions.*

* * *

***Tugs are usually available** at most of the major ports on the Great Lakes. With advance notice, they can usually be obtained for smaller ports as well.*

* * *

*The state of Michigan, in conjunction with local communities, has constructed a series of **small-craft harbors of refuge** along the Michigan shorelines. Usually they are no more than 20 miles apart, except on Lake Superior, where they may be as much as 40 miles apart.*

* * *

***The Great Lakes System** includes Lakes Ontario, Erie, Huron, Michigan and Superior, their connecting waterways, and the St. Lawrence River.. it is one of the largest concentrations of fresh water on the earth.*

* * *

From the Straight of Belle Isle at the mouth of the Gulf of St. Lawrence, the distance via the St. Lawrence River to

Duluth, Minnesota, at the head of Lake Superior is about 2,340 miles, and to Chicago, Illinois, near the S end of the Lake Michigan is about 2,250 miles. About 1,000 miles of each of these distances is below Montreal, the head of deep-draft navigation on the St. Lawrence River.

* * *

It is said that Lake Superior was discovered in 1629 by a French explorer named Etienne Brule. Jean Nicolet discovered Michigan in 1634, and in 1669, Joliet discovered Lake Erie. But the first recognized discoverer of the Lakes was by Samuel de Champlain when, in 1615, he and his explorers arrived at Lake Huron on French Creek.

* * *

In the beginning, charts were rough. Champlain, it is said, made the first one of the Lakes in 1632. But in addition to being inaccurate, it was incomplete, showing only Huron, Ontario and Superior. Those were the only ones he knew about.

* * *

In 1852, the United States Lake Survey printed and issued the first Great Lakes charts. But a more complete series was issued in 1882.

* * *

Lake Superior contains the deepest water of the four lakes— 1,300 feet.

* * *

The first steam whistle heard on the Great Lakes *was reportedly on the steamboat ROCHESTER, which ran out of Buffalo. It is said that its captain was perusing a foreign newspaper when he discovered crude plans for a steam whistle. His plan to build a workable model succeeded, and he sounded it just as the ROCHESTER and GENERAL PORTER were entering the Straights of Mackinac. The sound was frightening the crew of the latter, and it dropped back, enabling the ROCHESTER to arrive in port first.*

* * *

By intergovernmental agreement between the United States and Canada, the waters of the Great Lakes and the St. Lawrence River have been divided into designated and undes-

ignated waters for pilotage purposes. In designated waters, registered vessels of the U.S. and foreign vessels are required to have in their service a U.S.- or Canadian-registered pilot.

Lake Superior, *with a coastline of 1,500 miles,* **has an average depth of 475 feet** *and has a maximum depth of 1,290 feet. It has some bays, peninsulas and islands. The larger bays are Thunder, Black, Nipigon and Heron on the north coast, and Chequamegon, Whitefish and Keweenaw on the south. The Keweenaw Peninsula of Upper Michigan is the largest in the lake.*

* * *

Islands of size *include Isle Royale, St. Ignace, Simpson, Michipicoten, Cooper, Grand, Manitou and Slate, and the group of Apostle Islands.*

* * *

Superior, *with a drainage basin of 80,900 square miles—some 37,570 square miles of them are in the United States—* **drains southward** *into Lake Huron via the 62-mile length of the St. Marys River.*

* * *

The most important cities on Lake Superior *are Thunder Bay (formerly Fort Williams and Port Arthur), Nipigon, Michipicoten, and Saulte Ste. Marie, Ontario; Saulte Ste. Marie and Marquette, Mich.; Superior and Ashland, Wis.; and Duluth and Two Harbors, Minn.*

* * *

Superior, *like the other Great Lakes,* **was formed by the action of glaciers.**

* * *

Some types of vessels, called **bulk carriers, are designed to carry dry bulk cargoes** *such as grain, coal, sulfur, stone and ore. Considered the most distinctive and numerous of this general type are the bulk freighters of the Great Lakes. With their engines located far aft and their pilothouse on the forecastle, some of these vessels now have reached 1,000 feet in length. Early on, they carried no gear for loading or unloading, and depended upon dockside assistance. Later, the self-unloaders were developed, now making it possible for* *ships leaving the Great Lakes via the St. Lawrence Seaway to offload into larger vessels with their own equipment as opposed to paying for that service to be performed by a third party.*

* * *

*The **savings made possible by using self-unloaders** at one time facilitated the shipment of Powder River Basin coal from Wyoming to Europe via the Great Lakes and Seaway at a price almost equal to that charged for moving coal by barge down the Mississippi. And the cargo traveled a shorter distance.*

* * *

*Local **magnetic disturbances** are more prevalent on Lake Superior than on the other Great Lakes. The strongest, according to reports by vessel masters, are along the north shore of the lake. They decrease in intensity as the distance between the vessel and this shore increases. The tendency is for upbound vessels to be drawn toward the north shore.*

Superstitions And Sea Talk

St. Elmo's fire, an electrical manifestation, was not understood by ancient mariners It is produced when the electricity of a low-hanging cloud combines with that of the earth. Mariners of old thought of St. Elmo as Saint Erasmus, whom superstitious European sailors called upon to protect them from storms. They called the fire Castor and Pollux, who Greek mythology tells us were twin brothers who rode about on white horses, appearing with aid in times of distress.

* * *

Quite common in sailing tales of old, being relived through modern movies, is the myth about **women aboard** ship being **a bad omen**. Whether she be a captain's wife or not, the woman was thought to be very unlucky for the ship and its crew.

* * *

In the old days of sailing, from the time of the Egyptian galleys, **a coin was placed on the keelson under the maststep** to provide the ship goodluck.

* * *

Davy Jones, according to the beliefs of sailors, is a friend who presides over all of the evil spirits of the deep. Thus the reference to Davy Jones' Locker.

* * *

When the helmsman was requested to **"give me some leeway,"** it meant he should leave adequate room between the ship and an object on the windward side. Nowadays we make our request for space by saying "cut me some slack."

* * *

When vessels are ready to leave the shipyard proper and be put into the water, care is always taken to **"grease the ways"** to make the trip down the marine ways a smooth one.

Where The Boats Are

In old days, any cannon shot beyond 50 yards was considered a **"long shot."** These days we use the term to mean that the "odds are against us"—the possibility of accomplishing our taks is not very good.

* * *

The term **"under the weather"** grew out of the sailor's confrontation with the elements. Today it would probably be used most often to indicate someone is ailing.

* * *

Today we think of a **figurehead** as a person holding a position for symbolic purposes only. In olden days, however, the figurehead was ornate and was placed on the bows of ships to ward off evil spirits. Later, as mariners became less superstitious, the figureheads were thought of in an ornamental sense.

* * *

When the booms used to load cargo ships have completed their work and ar lowered, it is known as **"lowering the boom."** The term is used in modern days to mean to put an end to something, or perhaps come down hard on someone. Remember in the song how "Clancy lowered the boom"?

* * *

Today, the **"smoking lamp"** is being put out all over the world because of the danger of smoke to health. Sailors of old could not smoke just whenever they wished either. But their concern was for the safety of the ship. A fire at sea is terrible thing. Thus, in order to combat one of their worst fears, the sailor had access to flame only at the 'smoking lamp," where he could smoke when "it was lit." He could not go elsewhere to smoke.

* * *

Alcohol was a problem in days of old just as it is today, and a sailor who was **"three sheets to the wind"** was one who had consumed enough to be out of control. Sheets are the lines used to trim sails to the wind. If three were broken, it could render a sailing ship uncontrollable."

* * *

"Sailing under false colors" was a practice used by some pirates to entice victim ships within range. As depicted in movies, as the intended target was close enough, the pirates hoisted the "Jolly Roger"—the black flag carrying upon it a white skull and crossbones.

Maritime & Transportation Terms

A1—a first-class vessel. The letter "A" stands for the class in which the hull is scheduled. The one refers to the stores and equipment.

Abaft—refers to a location near the stern of a vessel.

Abandonment—in water transportation this refers to constructive total loss.

Aboard—in nautical terms meaning on or in a ship. It is used by other modes of transportation as well.

ABS—American Bureau of Shipping, a vessel classification agency that assigns international loadlines.

Admeasure—to measure, calculate, and certify the dimensions of a vessel and its gross and net tons for registration purposes.

Admiralty—used in connection with marine matters. Also refers to jurisdiction over causes of action occuring in connection with contracts to transport goods by water.

Admiralty Court—a court that has jurisdiction over legal disputes arising out of navigation on public waters.

Affreightment—a contract to move cargo in which the cargo owner/shipper is neither charterer nor operator of the vessel.

AIWW—Atlantic Intracoastal Waterway.

Anchorage—a spot near shore where ships are in safety.

Anchor billboard—a structure on the deck of a vessel upon which the anchor is mounted when not in use.

Anodes—metallic plates, which when attached to the hull of a vessel, decompose because of electrolysis, thereby reducing deterioration of hull plate.

Ballast—anything other than cargo, placed aboard a ship to achieve the desired draft or trim.

Bareboat charter—a vessel that is chartered without a crew is referred to as a "bareboat" charter.

Beam—the greatest width of a ship.

Bearings of a vessel—the waterline at its widest part when in trim.

Bell book—a book to record the time and signal of engine orders.

Bilge—the lower inner space of a vessel's hull.

Bitt—(also sometimes referred to bollard or timberhead)—a single or double post, either on a vessel or on a wharf, to which lines are secured.

Blanks—any number of shipping forms (vouchers, weigh bills, bills of lading, etc.).

Bollard pull—the static pulling force of a tugboat measured in pounds.

Bow—the front end of a vessel. (The bow is also referred to as the forward end.)

Boxed end—the end of a barge that is squared for its full width and depth.

Breakwater—a structure that provides protection from the sea.

Bridle—A V-shaped chain, wire or rope that is attached to a vessel to which a towline is connected.

Brokers—people who either lease out their own equipment, or arrange for the purchase and resale of marketable goods. Or it could be a person who serves as a ship agent, locating cargo and doing other business for the ship.

Bulwark—that side of a vessel that extends above the upper deck.

Buoy—a stationary floating object used as an aid to navigation.

Cabotage—a term referring to the shipment of cargo between ports of a nation.

Camel—a pontoon used to fender between two vessels or a vessel and a wharf. Frequently referred to as a sea camel in bluewater ports.

Carriage of Goods at Sea Act—U.S. laws that cover ocean carrier loss and damage obligations.

Channel—that portion of a waterway that is naturally deep or is artifically deepened in order to use it for navigation.

Chocks—in the maritime industry, are metal castings through which lines may be passed for mooring or towing.

Cleat—a metal fitting, with two protection fittings, around which lines may be fastened. (Small ones are even found useful in households.)

Cofferdam—a space in a vessel between two closely located parallel bulkheads. On the inland waterways (rivers) it refers to a temporary dam constructed of sheet-pile cells, located closely together to hold back the river during construction projects.

Deadman—an object such as anchor, piling or concrete block buried ashore and to which other structures may be attached for support.

Deadweight tonnage (dwt.)—a vessel's cargo capacity.

Docking tug—a vessel that is used to assist large sea-going vessels to and from their berths.

Draft—the depth of a boat's keel below the waterline.

Draft Marks—numbers at the side of a vessel at bow and stern to indicate the amount of water the vessel draws.

Drydocking—removing a vessel from the water to repair it.

Dumb vessel—any vessel that cannot be moved under its own power.

Dunnage—any type of material used to block or brace cargo.

ETA—estimated time of arrival.

ETD—estimated time of departure.

Fender—a device strategically positioned to absorb shock between a vessel and another object.

F.O.B.—cargo delivered to and placed aboard a carrier at a specific point free of charge.

Freeboard—the distance from the waterline to the main deck of a vessel.

Gale—a wind of 35 to 65 mph. and having a varying intensity.

General ship—a vessel whose owner operates the ship and carries cargo for anyone who applies.

GIWW—Gulf Intracoastal Waterway, extends from Brownsville, Texas, to Florida.

Gross tonnage—the volume measurement of the internal voids of a vessel wherein 100 cubic feet equals one ton.

Gross ton (G.T.)—a long ton, 2,240 pounds.

Gross ton-mile—the movement of transportation equipment and its cargo one mile.

Gunwale—that part of a vessel where the side and the main deck meet.

Harbor boat—any powered vessel used primarily in harbor operations.

Hatch—a removable cover over the cargo hold of a vessel.

Hawser—heavy line used for mooring, towing or securing a vessel to the dock.

Hull—that main portion of a vessel that provides flotation.

Kevel (or caval)—heavy metal deck fitting having two horn-shaped projections around which lines can be made fast for mooring or towing a vessel.

Knot—one nautical mile per hour.

Lighter—vessel used to load or unload a ship.

Lines—the ropes or cables (steel wires) used to tow or moor vessels or for lashings.

Logs—the official records of the day-to-day operations of a manned vessel.

Manhole—an opening in the deck, generally to provide access for a person.

MarAd—the U.S. Maritime Administration.

Master—a vessel's captain.

MRGO—Mississippi River-Gulf Outlet.

Nautical mile—is a unit of length used in sea navigation It is equal to 1,852 meters—about 6,076 feet.

Navigable waterways—waters upon which commercial and private vessels are able to operate in their usual mode of navigation.

Net tons—the gross tons of a vessel after having made deductions for certain specified non-cargo spaces.

Rules of the Road—a code governing the operation of vessels.

Running lights—those lights required to be shown aboard a vessel that is underway at night.

Sailing line—the preferred course for safe and efficient navigation.

Seaworthy—generally means that a vessel is reasonably fit for navigation, that it can carry cargo and crew safely. However, of late, if Coast Guard rules are violated, a vessel can be considered "unseaworthy" for legal purposes. An example might be failure to keep in the pilothouse navigation charts or other documents required by the Coast Guard.

Sheer—the upward curvature of a vessel's deck at the bow or stern.

Starboard—the right hand side of a vessel when facing forward. (The left hand side is the port side. An easy way to distinguish between port and starboard is to remember that port wine is red wine. Also, when vessels are returning to port, mariners keep in mind: red right returning, which means when you are returning to port, the red buoys or red lights will be to your right.)

Stern—the after or rear end of a vessel.

Strake—a transverse row of steel hull plates.

Superstructure—the structural part of a vessel above the main deck.

Survey—a critical examination of a vessel, cargo or marine structure.

Surveyor—a qualified marine inspector.

Time charter—a contract for services of a vessel for a specified length of time. During this period, the primary control and management of the vessel remain with the owner.

Tow—to push or pull vessel(s) on a waterway.

Towboat—any powered vessel used for towing. (Depending upon the location, some refer to them as pushboats.)

VCG—vertical center of gravity, a vital computation used in determing the stability of a vessel.

Wheel—another term for propeller. (Vessels with two wheels are frequently referred to as having twin screws.)

WQIS—Water Quality Insurance Syndicate, an underwriting agency formed by insurance companies to insure against losses resulting from water pollution.

Afterword

By this point, all of you should be experts on Great Lakes shipping, and in finding boats at Duluth-Superior and Thunder Bay! At least, I hope to have answered a few questions, and stimulated an interest in watching the big boats come and go. Once you start exploring around the Twin Ports and Lakehead, I feel sure you'll be back. You may come up with something new of interest that I haven't covered. If so, I would appreciate hearing from you. Address correspondence to me in care of the publisher's address in the front of the book.

Lake Superior and the boats that cross her waters mean many things to many people. To some, being on the lake is a job, just part of their workaday life. Many people who have worked on the boats all of their lives show little interest in the lake or shipping, which always seems a little strange to me. Lake Superior symbolizes vacation time for many people, a place to relax, fish, and sail. To still others, the lake is a spiritual place, that helps them find inner peace and joy.

The thrill of seeing the harbor and Lake Superior in her many moods is an experience in itself. You can live your entire life here, and still capture the lake in a new character. Cool, crystal clear summer and fall days, foggy spring mornings when mist softens the shore but makes the lake a white hell for the boats, and violent nor'easter gales that seem to come out of nowhere, are all part of the Lake Superior experience. If you are a seasoned boatwatcher, you already understand this experience. If not, I invite you to spend a day, a weekend, or a week or more at the "Head of the Lakes" or the "Land of the Sleeping Giant," and find out for yourself!

J. A. Baumhofer

Boatwatchers' Log

The following pages provide a log to record your tour, the vessels you see, weather conditions, and any other pertinent information that will help you remember your tour.

Tour Notes ... ...

Date:	Time:	Site:

Tour Notes ... ...

Date:	Time:	Site:

Tour Notes ... ...

Date: Time: Site:

Tour Notes ... ...

Date: Time: Site:

Tour Notes ... ...

Date: Time: Site:

Tour Notes ... ...

Date: Time: Site:

Tour Notes ... ...

Date: Time: Site:

Tour Notes ... ...

Date: Time: Site:

Tour Notes ... ...

Date: Time: Site:

Tour Notes ... ...

Date: Time: Site:

Tour Notes ... ...

Date: Time: Site:

J. A. Baumhofer

Tour Notes ... ...

Date: Time: Site:

Tour Notes ... ...

Date: Time: Site:

Tour Notes ... ...

Date: Time: Site:

Tour Notes ... ...

Date: Time: Site:

Tour Notes ... ...

Date: Time: Site:

Tour Notes ... ...

Date: Time: Site: